THE
TRAIN
HOME

By Susan Richards Shreve

Nᴀɴ A. Tᴀʟᴇꜱᴇ

DOUBLEDAY

NEW YORK

LONDON

TORONTO

SYDNEY

AUCKLAND

THE
TRAIN
HOME

Susan Richards
Shreve

PUBLISHED BY NAN A. TALESE
an imprint of Doubleday,
a division of
Bantam Doubleday Dell Publishing Group, Inc.
1540 Broadway, New York, New York 10036

DOUBLEDAY and the portrayal of an anchor
with a dolphin are trademarks of
Doubleday, a division of Bantam Doubleday Dell
Publishing Group, Inc.

Book Design by Gretchen Achilles

ISBN 0-385-42357-8

To *T.S.*

"True religion, in spirit, is a sense of the heart."
from Jonathan Edwards

Will Huston—not Father James as he was calling himself for the purposes of this visit to the United States—but Will Huston of Dublin, member of the Abbey Theatre Co., playwright, lately failed playwright, closed the door of locker A270 at Union Station in Washington, D.C., and slid the key in his shoe.

In the locker, he had left his knapsack with two dress shirts, a pair of trousers, a change of underclothes, and papers which identified him as William Huston of 115 Archduke Street, Dublin—his passport, his driver's license, and three photographs: one of Maud O'Connor taken at his mother's flat, one of his father as an altar boy in 1931, and a picture taken of his brother Jamey in Belfast.

He went to the crowded men's room in the main lobby of the station—several men at the sinks, the urinals in use with a line of men waiting. Will went into a cubicle, locked the door, set his small valise on the back of the toilet, and opened it.

He had taken the priest's robe from the costume room at the Abbey Theatre the night before he left Dublin, taken as well a silver-gray wig with straight hair somewhat longer than his own. He put on the black cassock and the wig and made a small cut on his upper right cheek with makeup he had taken from the Abbey dressing room to use in the event of an emergency. Then he sat down on the toilet seat and waited. He did not want the men who might have noticed him arrive as a civilian to see his conversion.

At the newsstand, he bought a copy of the *Washington Post,* a bag of chocolate-covered peanuts, a toothbrush, a package of Marlboro cigarettes, and inquired for directions by subway to Dupont Circle.

The car was empty except for an elderly woman in the seat across from his, her white hair held off her forehead by a large black satin bow as if she were a schoolgirl, and a boy in torn blue jeans, seated sideways on the seat, his feet stretched out, blowing pink gum bubbles which exploded in little pops across his lips.

Will checked his watch. It was four-thirty and he had told the receptionist at Lacey House on R Street he would be arriving at four o'clock exactly.

That morning, he had left from his cousin's apartment in Manhattan.

"For New Jersey," he'd told Brendan, to visit his Uncle Patrick, his father's younger brother, for a few days before he went back to Dublin on Friday. But at Penn Station, he'd bought a coach ticket for Washington, D.C.

He adjusted the starched white collar against his neck and opened the *Washington Post* for Tuesday, November 19, 1991. The doors to the car remained open although there were no passengers on the platform and the air was too warm.

"Why doesn't the train go, Father?" the boy with the bubble gum asked Will.

"I surely don't know," Will said.

"I'm late," the boy said crossly, although he did not appear to be the kind of boy with appointments. "I'm very late."

Just then, a girl or young woman rushed into the car carrying an enormous bag, with a backpack over her shoulder. She had dark hair, straight under a red cloth hat, dark eyes, a dancer or perhaps an athlete by her carriage. Maybe Spanish, Will thought.

She stopped and looking around the nearly empty train headed straight for the seat in front of Will as if she had a mission.

2

Annie Blakemore fled down the escalator of the Union Station subway, taking the moving steps two at a time, through the turnstile and still at a run onto the Red Line train to Shady Grove just before the doors shut.

The train was not crowded—several empty double seats ahead—but when she checked, running her eyes down the aisle, there in the fourth seat back by the window looking directly at her was a priest, boyish but not young, with gray hair long over the collar. The look he gave her was not flirtatious, although she had reason to be suspicious of priests, but rather inquiring, as if they knew one another and her sudden appearance on the subway alarmed him.

Later, when she went over their meeting, over and

over their meeting, which would, in the eyes of another, less hopeful woman, have been insignificant, she would say to herself, even aloud if no one was around to hear her:

"My heart stopped when I saw him."

And though her heart did not exactly stop of course, something happened to Annie Blakemore, a conversion or a vision, something of sufficient magnitude to lay claim to her imagination whose wide range had already shown the capacity to escape the life of her birth.

She sat down in the seat in front of him, her back to the window so she could see him, pressing between the seats the shopping bag with her costume for Despina in Mozart's *Così Fan Tutte*.

"I'll do the alterations," she'd said to the costume mistress that afternoon when she got the news that Marcia had fallen ill with flu, giving Annie her first chance at a solo role in the Washington Opera for which she was a cover in case of an emergency.

"No, no, no," the costume mistress had said. "For tonight you are a solo. You must learn to behave important."

But Annie took the costume anyway, sewed it up in the bathroom of the Duke Ellington School of the Arts during her lunch break, went to the shops at Union Station after class to buy high-heeled shoes, and now she had just over two hours to get home, feed the children, get a sitter, iron the costume, wash her hair, and be at the Kennedy Center by seven.

The priest had olive eyes flecked with yellow and fine high cheekbones—she noticed them immediately in the bright interior lights of the subway—a dark caste to his face, gray-black under the eyes, an angry scar, very small and still raw, just above the cheekbone.

Annie was a quick observer. She had, as Adam used to tell her before his accident, mercury for a brain. She liked that, growing up as she had in a family in which the brain was not considered a necessary part of the human equipment.

Annie smiled at the priest but his face, somber in repose, registered no response and she was suddenly self-conscious. She was not inclined to be forward with strangers, although certainly she would be described as forward by those few people who had known her since childhood.

There were things she wanted, unimaginable in the life of a migrant worker's daughter, the daughter of a pool shark, a drunk. She was not possessed of the kind of wit necessary to negotiate favors but she did believe that anything was possible for a girl with a certain talent as she had and the luck of a mercury brain.

Where she'd come by such faith, there was no telling.

Sometimes in reproduction, there is an accident of nature, a kind of genetic mutation of the spirit, and the coupling throws off a complete surprise. Annie was that kind of surprise—born Dolores Ann Grainey, Delirious Grainey was the name her father, on one of his long drunks, gave to the people at the birth and death office in Oklahoma City, and so her birth certificate still read. Delirious Ann Grainey, born in Sidle, Oklahoma, May 11, 1951, 6 lbs. 1 oz. They'd moved to Sidle a month or two before Annie's birth, then on to Arkansas when she was three months old, then Texas. Wanderers, the Graineys, always packing up. She was the eighth child, fourth daughter of Rebecca and Millard "Ace" "Fighting Bull" Grainey —"Ace" for his skill at pool, "Fighting Bull" to prove him by name if not by blood kin to the Cherokee in Oklahoma where he'd grown up.

"The last child," Rebecca said to Ace when Annie was born. "The eighth and last."

The priest's hands—at least his left hand—gripped the seat in front of him, actually gripped it so his knuckles were white as if he had advance notice of a subway accident and was prepared. In his other hand he held the *Washington Post* rolled up, a small paper bag, and an unlit cigarette.

She wished to tell him that she was susceptible to priests, that she was now Catholic, had converted to Catholicism when she was thirteen, living in Paris where everyone was Catholic. Which had been true, of course, that everyone was Catholic, but that had been Brammel, Texas, in the Mexican neighborhood, not Paris, the year she got her first job taping cars at Al's body shop to save money for braces so she could get her teeth fixed since the choir director at First Baptist Brammel said she had the voice of an angel and could have a career on the American stage.

"Excuse me," Annie said. "Do you know what stop is Tenley?"

"I'm terribly sorry," the priest said, a small smile lighting his eyes—enough of a smile, in any case, for Annie's heart to race. He had an accent, quite a heavy one, which sounded Irish but with his silver-gray hair and dark angular face, he didn't have the look of other Irish people she had known. Certainly not pale-skinned Adam Blakemore.

At Metro Center, the train filled, people crowded in the aisles. The priest stood to give an older woman his seat, so Annie stood as well, pulling her shopping bag from between the seats.

She checked her watch, four forty-seven, slid behind a tall man in a blue polyester suit, shiny she noticed, dandruff on his shoulders, down his back. When the doors opened, she got off the subway four stops before Tenleytown, where she lived in the 3300 block of Fessenden Street in a blue shingle house and where, at this moment, Alexandra and Nicholas Blakemore would be waiting for her to come home. They did not go alone into the house, although they were old enough certainly to cope with Adam—Alexandra eight at the end of the month, Nicholas already six.

Annie threaded her way through the large crowd at Dupont Circle, slipped her fare card into the slot of the turnstile, keeping the priest in view.

She was not by nature suggestible, too much in retreat

from her childhood, too guarded against her fear of being discovered as Dolores Ann Grainey of Brammel, Texas, against the dangers of her life with Adam Blakemore. But this clear November afternoon, stirred by the excitement of a chance to sing her own aria, dreaming of escape, Annie was susceptible or she would not have allowed herself the flight of imagination to follow a strange priest off the subway at Dupont Circle, to actually believe something could happen between them.

The priest was quite a distance ahead of her, on the escalator, walking at a clip up the moving steps. She took off after him, keeping the long black skirt of his robe in view as the dark tunnel of the subway opened to the twilight on Dupont Circle. She saw him cross the street, stop at a public telephone on the corner, and make a call. She waited by the fruit vendor, bought a banana and an apple, stuck them in the shopping bag with her costume, but by the time she looked up he had disappeared. She ran to the corner. He was not walking down R Street, nor did she spot him on the sidewalks of Connecticut Avenue in either direction, and then he came out of a tobacco store, turned right at R, and she waited until he was halfway down the block to follow.

R Street was empty except for a Catholic schoolgirl in a blue plaid uniform and lipstick, a bookbag over her shoulder, smoking a cigarette.

''Do you have a dollar for the subway?'' she asked Annie as she passed.

Annie shook her head.

"Fuck you," the girl said under her breath.

The priest was in the second block, no one between them, when he stopped. Annie slipped behind a tree. She saw him reach under his robe, take out a piece of paper, look at the row of houses, and walk up the steps of a yellow brick house with black wrought iron. By the time she reached the house, the priest had disappeared inside. 2115 R Street, she said to herself and then, extremely late already, she ran down 21st Street and back to Q toward the Dupont Circle subway and home.

The doors on the Metro closed behind Annie and she stood until Tenleytown, her cheeks flushed with excitement. 2115 R Street, she said to herself. She moved between two women talking and took hold of the rail.

She wondered what the priest had thought of her.

"You are not beautiful exactly," Adam had said to her before their only trip to Brammel, Texas, to visit the Grainey family. "You are beautiful inexactly."

And Annie should have known then that she did not measure up, should not have bothered to take Adam to Brammel at all. She should have told him good-bye after the road tour of *The Fantastiks* and sent him off to the scrubbed Connecticut town where he was born.

Alexandra and Nicholas were waiting on the front porch when Annie arrived. They were actually lying on the porch, head to head, with their eyes closed, Nicholas's small red tongue hanging out of his mouth as if he were ill.

She leaned down and kissed them on their foreheads.

"Guess what?" she said stepping across Alexandra whose eyes were still closed. "Marcia has the flu and I'm singing tonight." She nudged Alexandra with her foot. "Up up up. We've got to hurry."

"We thought you were dead," Alexandra said. "We thought you had fallen in front of a subway and been squished." She opened her eyes and looked at her mother out of Adam's bright blue eyes. "You're forty minutes late. I've been checking my watch."

"Alexandra said you'd been kidnapped," Nicholas said.

"Well, I wasn't kidnapped today," Annie said.

"People are going to think your children are insane," Adam's mother had said to him just this summer when they were visiting at the Blakemores' farm in Connecticut.

"They are insane," Adam said, amused. "Insanity runs in Annie's family."

"I thought alcoholism ran in your family, Annie," Gail Blakemore said. "No one has ever mentioned the insanity to me."

"My children have large imaginations," Annie said defensively. "They listen to opera," she said. "I read them the librettos."

"What do you think, Adam?" Mrs. Blakemore asked.

"I don't know what to say, Mother. The children are Annie's," Adam said. "Immaculately conceived."

Annie opened the front door and dumped her shopping bag and backpack in the hall. The house was airless and smelled of cat pee as it usually did when Adam was home all day, refusing to let the cats out or to answer the telephone, playing the all-news station at top volume as it was playing now. She opened the window next to the piano since it was warm for November and picked up the telephone to call Sara Ponder, who was usually willing to stay with the children in spite of Adam.

"Don't call Sara," Alexandra said quietly when Annie picked up the phone. "Take us with you."

"It's a school night, darling," Annie said. "Not on a school night."

"We are afraid to stay with Papa," Alexandra said.

Nicholas nodded from the floor where he was dumping his reading books from his book bag. "Yesterday he was terrible." He looked up at his mother.

"I know," Annie said hanging up the telephone before it rang in the Ponder house.

Annie hardly tried with Adam any longer. She kept the house sunny and open, the windows cleaned. She had flowers in the living room and made bright curtains, baked cookies on the weekend, lemon cakes for Sunday supper. She imitated the pictures of family lives in the magazines at the checkout counter of the Safeway. She covered the beds in quilts, kept potpourri in bowls on the windowsills to get rid of the smell of the cats, Brunnhilde and Siegfried, played Mozart on the stereo, and had made a tiny library in a corner of the kitchen so she and Nicholas and Alexandra had a place to go after dinner when Adam filled the living room with his black temper.

She was not unhappy. "Lighthearted" was how her friends at Ellington described her, and certainly she was the most cheerful member of the Company of the Washington Opera. But lighthearted was not an accurate description. What Annie Blakemore had was a quality of spirit, a kind of regenerative innocence about the human condition. And faith in possibilities.

"For vacation, we might go to Paris," she'd tell Nicholas and Alexandra. "We'll take a tiny apartment on the Île de la Cité and drink coffee in the cafés," she'd say. "Or maybe Africa if we can save a lot of money. And see the wonderful animals."

"Are we really going someplace for Christmas vacation?" Nicholas, more literal-minded than his sister, would ask.

"We're going to Texas," Alexandra said. "And get to see Aunt Sylvie in jail."

"We've already been to Texas too much," Nicholas said sadly. "We never go to the places you promise, Mama. Just Texas."

"Someday," Annie said cheerfully.

"Someday, after Adam," Alexandra said.

Annie had never thought about "after Adam" until recently. Since their summer visit with the Blakemores in Essex, there had been an alteration in Adam, as if he had suffered a neurological event and the anger sunk in the deep pockets of his brain was free to roam the house.

Sometimes Annie was afraid of him.

Now she knocked on the bedroom door. He was sitting by the window, his dark red hair unkempt, his robe open to the chest, a handsome man still in spite of his lack of self-regard. He was writing and did not look up.

"Marcia is ill tonight and I'm singing," Annie said.

"That's a very nice opportunity for you, Delirious," he said.

He had started to call her Delirious that past summer in Connecticut right after her father had died of liver failure. At first it was very funny, the way Adam said it—Delirious—matter-of-factly, as if the name were an ordinary Christian name. But he'd kept on through the fall and now there was an edge, a kind of madness.

"I'm taking the children with me," she said and closed the door before he could reply.

Later, in the shower, the streams of hot water pouring down her cheeks, over her stomach, her thighs, the priest from the subway appeared, standing in his long black robe and bare feet, catching the water from Annie's nipples with his tongue.

3

Will Huston was struck by the young woman on the subway. "Adorable" had been his father's word for the women he particularly liked, and that was how Will would think of her later, trying to put out of mind his mission in Washington, to fall asleep in the hard bed of the Lacey Guest House—"adorable," he thought, as if he were describing not a woman but a young girl on the edge of self-consciousness.

She must be a dancer or an actress—not only in her carriage, which he had noticed when she walked onto the subway, but in the way she tilted her head in her red cloth hat, the way a galaxy of emotions shimmered on the surface of her face with too much intensity for a brief encounter.

. . .

The subway stopped at Metro Center and filled up, so Will stood to give a seat to others. He avoided glancing at the young woman because he could feel her eyes on him as if she had suddenly guessed the purpose of his visit to Washington or knew by intuition that he was not a priest.

"Dupont Circle," the loudspeaker called out and Will moved toward the exit doors, through the crowded platform, up the long moving stairs—like London, the length of them—and out onto Dupont Circle.

From a public telephone on the corner, he called the British embassy and asked for the Washington address of Michael Maguire.

"I'll give you Mr. Maguire's secretary," the woman who answered the telephone said.

Will identified himself as Mr. Suter of the Washington office of Grady, Simpson and Loew, names he made up on the spot.

"I'm calling for Mr. Maguire's home address to post him an invitation to a party," Will said.

"He's on the other line, Mr. Suter," the secretary said in a friendly manner, as if they were familiar associates.

"Don't bother him," Will said pleasantly. "I only need the address."

She hesitated. "One moment please."

Perhaps addresses were protected. Certainly he would hang up if Michael Maguire came on the line or if the secretary came back to him with more questions.

"3524 Reservoir Road. 20007 is the zip code," the secretary said and hung up the telephone before he had an opportunity to thank her.

Lacey House was a small guest house for visiting priests. There were twelve rooms, a small dining room where only breakfast was served, and a parlor where at the time of Will's arrival two young priests, Americans with broad northern accents, were speaking of visits to the Vatican. Will nodded to the priests, unsmiling, not wishing for conversation, and followed the young receptionist to the room on the third floor, number 11, where he would be staying for the duration of his visit in Washington. The room was small, for which she apologized, but his reservations had come only the night before, she said. There were two windows side by side without curtains overlooking an alley, a single bed with a white chenille spread, a bureau with quite a small mirror over it—disappointing since he would have liked to see himself as a priest full length. There was a small desk, no telephone, and he shared a bath, which could be, he thought, inconvenient depending on the turn of events.

By the time he had unpacked his nightshirt, his missal, the pack of cigarettes and opened the entertainment section of the *Washington Post* hoping to find a play so he could busy himself for the sake of his nerves, it was after five o'clock.

According to the newspaper, there was a performance of *A Wonderful Life* at the Arena, a play by August Wilson at the Eisenhower, *A Christmas Carol* at the Ford, and *Così Fan*

Tutte at the Opera House of the Kennedy Center. The opera was his preference, he decided, folding the newspaper, tossing it in the trashbin. He did not read the national news on the front page of the *Post,* only the headlines, and could not ever read bad news of a personal nature reported in the metropolitan section of city newspapers—children hit by buses, apartment fires, a girl murdered in the park. He did have an interest in the obituaries of strangers, measuring his own life against the attrition of Irishmen, noting their reported age in the *Dublin Times,* the manner of death.

He was peculiar about news stories. After his little brother Jamey died, he could not read of the disasters which struck the lives of real people. Only the lives of fictional characters, the fates of people fixed in place, unalterable by a sudden turn of events.

Downstairs at Lacey House, he asked the receptionist about the opera and how he could go about getting tickets and whether there was a place to have supper nearby. She made a telephone call and said there were only standing room tickets for ten dollars; an Italian restaurant, Domenico's, was near the Kennedy Center.

On R Street, he hailed a taxi.

"3524 Reservoir Road," he told the driver. "I'd like to go there first and then to the Kennedy Center."

"I can't wait for you," the driver said without expression.

"Never mind," Will said. "There's no need to wait. I'm just driving by to see where the house is."

"I'll have to charge you eight-fifty," the cabdriver said.

"Eight-fifty is fine," Will said. Tonight he simply wanted to see the house where Michael Maguire lived. He hoped to be sufficiently angered just by the sight of it, by the knowledge that Michael Maguire spent his nights there in a bed upstairs with Mrs. Maguire, unconcerned with the death of children.

He had not even thought about the details of his trip to Washington after his decision to come to America. He was not by nature interested in arrangements, too high-tempered for strategy. But he had a passion for the detail of character, for the way a story properly imagined should proceed. He was counting on that now.

Will had been imagining this trip for two months, since early September—September 11, in fact, the morning after the abrupt closing of his new play *Trenches*. At breakfast, he had read the *Belfast Times* which his mother sent to keep him up to date with the gossip in Belfast and the war. On the bottom of the third page of the front section was a small news clip reporting that Michael Maguire of London, formerly of Belfast, son of Esmé and Peter Maguire, now deceased, had been named second secretary of the British embassy in Washington, D.C.

"Do you happen to know the name Michael Maguire?" he had asked Maud who was making a pot of tea.

"Michael Maguire," Maud said.

She was still a pretty woman, although older than she looked, with the kind of soft face, beautiful at eighteen, which loses texture as it ages, sinks between the bones.

"I know the name Michael Maguire very well, of course." She put out a plate of biscuits. "There's Michael Maguire who has a sweet shop in Dublin near my mother's and Michael Maguire who went to grammar school with me and choked to death on a piece of apple. And Michael Maguire who is married to my cousin Nora. How many Michael Maguires do I need to name to please you, Will?"

He used to be fond of Maud's snappy replies, her quick tongue, but now he was on the edge of temper.

"Think," he said. He put the newspaper down so she could see the small notice on the bottom of the third page.

"You see? Son of Esmé and Peter Maguire, now deceased."

Maud looked blank. She poured hot water in the tea-pot and took milk out of the fridge.

"I don't know that Michael Maguire," she said sitting down heavily next to him.

"Yes you do. I have told you about him."

"You have?" She looked perplexed.

"That is the Michael Maguire who killed Jamey."

"No," Maud said softly. "It couldn't be."

"Yes it is," Will said. "Michael Maguire, son of Esmé and Peter Maguire. He is the same, risen from the dead."

"Was he dead?" Maud asked. "I thought he'd disappeared. That you'd lost track of him."

"I had," Will said. "You know that. I've told you the whole story hundreds of times. He disappeared two months after he killed Jamey." He got up from his chair. "I should have killed him then," he said. "If I'd known where to find him, I'd have killed him straightway." He poured himself a cap of whiskey, then another, lay down on the sofa in front of the television.

There had been a time when Will might have married Maud O'Connor but over the years their love affair had slipped away. What remained between them was the deep familiarity of siblings who live together waiting for a different future to announce itself.

"Don't talk of killing," Maud said passing him a biscuit. "Would you like a sandwich, Will? Shall we have lunch?"

"No," Will said. "I'm not ready to eat so soon."

Maud came in and sat at the end of the sofa.

"I'm sorry about Michael Maguire," she said.

"Pray he has terminal cancer," he said.

Will Huston was a warm, affectionate man, and for a character of dark introspection he had a way about him, a

23.

liveliness, a kind of genuine compassion. But for years, perhaps since Jamey's death, he had found no alleviation, except the temporary freedom he had in acting, from what he considered with a certain self-mockery a kind of suffering. The more he was engaged in matters of daily living, the more fragile he had become beneath the skin—like a man in an accident who must remain entirely still so the body can absorb the shock.

"So what are you going to do about Michael Maguire, now that you've found him?" Maud had asked Will that morning after the news in the Belfast paper.

"Nothing," Will replied. "Absolutely nothing. What could I do?"

But already, even dull-headed with whiskey, he was making plans.

"This is 3524," the cabbie said, slowing to a stop in front of a slender brick row house with a small porch and window boxes spilling dying white petunias. The house, very like the other houses on the block, was small, with shutters painted black and a garden in the front, neatly maintained. There was an elderly woman on the steps next to the Maguires' house making her way with a cane slowly to the street.

"You need to go in?" the cabbie asked.

"No," Will said. "Never mind."

"It seems a lot extra to pay just to look at a house," the cabbie said.

"I suppose it does," Will said pleasantly.

At the restaurant, he ordered squid and a bottle of white wine. He had planned to be disciplined, to drink half the bottle, a little more, but he drank it all and quickly. Though he was not drunk—Will was a regular drinker, a good-tempered one, and careful not to drink before performances—tonight the wine made him sleepy.

The theater was crowded, standing room only, with people lined up beside the rail of the orchestra section, against the wall at the back of the theater. By the time Will arrived, he had to stand without support during the whole first act, his head spinning. Standing in the hot theater, with a large crowd, his eyes closed, he could feel himself slipping to the floor and he caught the arm of the stranger on his left.

"I'm terribly sorry," Will said.

"You can have my place against the wall, Father," a young girl, just beyond where he had started to fall, said to him.

"That's very kind," he said.

"You can sit against the wall if you're tired," she suggested.

Will took her offer, pleased that she would think him tired and not drunk, which the gentleman whose arm he had grabbed must certainly have assumed. The wonder of children, he thought sitting against the wall, making his shoulders narrow so as not to take too much room.

"If you'd just let my brother sit here on the floor next to you," the little girl said. "He's extremely tired and not so fond of *Così Fan Tutte*."

The boy was smaller than the girl, no more than six, fair-haired and sweet-looking, and Will smiled to think that such a boy would have an opinion of *Così Fan Tutte*.

"Of course," he said moving to give the boy plenty of room.

The young girl stood just in front of him and turned not to the stage, where at the moment Fiordiligi was singing, but looked toward him directly until, unsettled by her scrutiny, he looked up and smiled. She was a lovely girl with a broad head, large eyes set far apart, and a stern expression on her face.

"I have never seen a priest at the opera," she said as if in criticism.

"Priests are often quite fond of opera," Will replied.

The girl folded her arms across her chest. "We're not supposed to talk in the theater," she said earnestly, as if Will had been the one to initiate conversation.

"Of course," Will whispered. "I apologize."

He closed his eyes. Fiordiligi had a lovely spring water voice, and it was agreeable to listen in a half sleep as he was doing when the boy against the wall next to him leaned hard against his arm.

"Father," he said in a loud whisper.

Will looked over. The boy had his hands between his legs holding his crotch.

"I have to pee," the boy said.

"Shh," the people standing beside them whispered.

"Shh, Nicholas," the girl said.

"I have to pee," the boy repeated.

"Nicholas, please," the girl said looking at Will in distress.

"I'll take him." Will struggled to get up.

Someone opened the door and the light from the lobby fell on the young girl's lovely face.

"Thank you, Father," she said politely.

"I always have to pee at the opera," the boy said as they walked down the thick maroon carpet. "And Alexandra always gets angry at me."

"You go to the opera often?" Will asked.

"Lots," the boy said, his hand still firmly on his crotch, as he followed Will down the corridor through the men's room door.

Something about the way the boy was walking, trotting really, or about his hair, square cut as Will's had been as a boy, or in the child's uncomplicated trust in a stranger, caught him by surprise. He took out a cigarette and smoked quickly to still his sudden nerves.

The little boy peed, washed his hands, and dried them on his trousers.

"We've missed Despina and Don Alfonso," the boy said.

"You know *Così Fan Tutte* very well, don't you?"

"I see every opera, especially if my mother is singing," he said, "but I like *Aida* best if they use real elephants."

"Your mother is singing tonight?" Will asked.

"She's Despina, but just for tonight," the boy said. "The real Despina is sick."

They walked back to the orchestra doors and had to wait until an aria was finished and then the usher, familiar with the boy, let them through the doors.

"You can read about my mother on a special piece of paper in the program if you want," the boy said.

"Thank you," Will said. "I will."

The boy sat with his sister against the back wall of the orchestra and this time Will stood. From time to time, he looked down at the boy, sleeping now, at the way his hair fell into a part, the way his small hands folded easily around his knees, and felt oddly comforted by the reassurance he gave of a normal world.

When the opera was over, Will lost the children. He wanted to say something to them, "Good-bye" or "It was a pleasure"—something ordinary.

He slid through the orchestra doors with the crowd, down the wide corridor of the Kennedy Center, and outside to a clear cool November night.

It was just after eleven, too early to go back to the

small room, the small bed at Lacey Guest House. He walked by the restaurant where he'd had dinner, then onto Virginia Avenue where he turned left following the reverse direction of the taxi which had brought him. He did not plan to return to Michael Maguire's house on Reservoir Road but he did just that, walking to M Street, past the rows of office buildings into the street noise of Georgetown. He felt an odd safety he had not felt since Jamey died.

At Wisconsin Avenue, Will turned right up the hill, past the Georgetown shops, the restaurants serving their last customers, the bars open with hostile teenagers lurking at the front doors, looking for action. Perhaps it was the protection of the robes of a priest, he thought as he crested the first hill of Wisconsin Avenue above the Potomac River. Perhaps this sense of well-being came of discovering a disguise. Who would harm a priest, after all? What was to be gained but a long purgatory? It occurred to him that he could remain a priest—a traveling priest on the road, place to place, all over the world. Good-bye to Maud and to his sisters and their husbands and their children. Good-bye, sweet Ireland. Good-bye. Light-footed he dashed up the last hill before Reservoir Road, turned left, overheated now from the brisk walk though the night was getting colder.

At the corner of 34th and Reservoir, he lit a cigarette, drew the smoke down his throat, and watched it cloud the air as he blew upwards. He could go to Australia,

New Zealand, Botswana, he thought. Father Grady slipping through the world. Perhaps he could, by a kind of osmosis, dressed as he was in the costume of a priest, believe in God again.

He crossed the street to the block where Michael Maguire lived. Ahead, half a block, a little more, a small car was pulling into a parking space and he picked up his pace, not wishing to be seen by the driver, a priest walking alone in a residential neighborhood at night. A woman got out of the passenger seat. She was small, with quite a lot of curly hair around her face. The door to the driver's side opened and a man got out, shutting the car door. He was beyond the circle of illumination from the streetlights so Will could not see him, but he could hear him speaking to his wife.

"Could you get my umbrella on the floor?" the man said; his accent was familiar. Will's heart quickened and he hurried to pass the car before the man came around the back into the light, before he had to see him. But he was too late. Michael Maguire stepped up on the curb in the full light of the streetlight, plumper than Will remembered, flushed, his pale red hair thin as baby hair on the top of his head. Surely it was Michael Maguire, although Will did not look long enough to identify him certainly.

Will walked by the Maguires' car with his head down, hearing their voices behind him; he did not stop until he was at the corner of the block. When he looked back,

Michael Maguire had gone into the house. He stopped then, half a block beyond the house, and leaned against a lamppost, his heart beating in his mouth, his blood running through his body, out his feet.

So that was Michael Maguire.

Michael Maguire of Belfast, Northern Ireland. Michael Maguire who had killed Jamey Huston on the thirteenth of July 1969. He went through the statistics to call to mind his reason for being on a street corner in Washington, D.C., so he wouldn't run as he felt like doing now. Run to Union Station. "Brendan," he'd say over the pay telephone in the station. "I'll be back in town tonight. I'll see you soon." He could take a plane to Dublin in the morning.

Michael Maguire. Will saw him now in the middle distance on Brendan's street in the Falls Road Section of Belfast, leading the cheering crowd toward Brendan's house —saw his red hair flying, his red face, his mouth open shouting something. Everyone in the crowd was shouting. This was the picture with which Will had lived for years like an abscess in the corner of his brain, and he called it back now to give him the courage to remain in Washington, to hold his ground as he had been doing since he made the decision to meet with Michael Maguire face to face that morning in Dublin after the closing of *Trenches*.

Jamey's death had not been an accident, not entirely an accident, for certainly when Michael Maguire fired the gun he was as close to Will as Will had been to him, close enough to recognize Will and Jamey Huston walking across Queen's Road to Brendan Mallory's cottage.

At MacArthur Boulevard, Will finally found an empty taxi. It was after one when he unlocked the front door of Lacey House and went up to his room. He took off his cassock and hung it over the desk chair. He took the program for *Così Fan Tutte* out of his pocket, some change, mostly quarters, a wad of bills.

His bed had been turned down and there was a pitcher of water on the desk, an apple and a pear, a container of soft yellow cheese wrapped in cellophane. He picked up the opera program, climbed into bed, and when he opened the program the sheet of information about the soprano who sang the role of Despina fell out.

For tonight, November 19, 1991, the role of Despina will be sung by Anna Blakemore, graduate of Northwestern University and Juilliard School of Music in voice. Ms. Blakemore is an occasional cover for the Washington Opera and a voice teacher at the Duke Ellington High School of the Arts. She began her career at Northwestern in musical theatre and then went on to study classical voice under Hays Brown at Juilliard. At Juilliard she sang the role of Adina in *L'Elisir d'Amore* and Susanna in *Le Nozze di*

Figaro. She has been on call for the Washington Opera Company since 1989.

Will turned out the light. Outside the windows there were sirens, one after the other, and it was too hot to sleep, as if the city just around the Lacey Guest House were on fire and he could not breathe in the thick air.

4

The lights were on in the house on Fessenden Street when Annie arrived by taxi just after midnight. All of the lights were on except the one in the upstairs bathroom and Annie's heart jumped. Adam kept the lights off when he was alone, even in the room where he was working, except for a small reading light over his manuscript.

"What do you think is the matter, Mama?" Alexandra asked.

Annie paid the driver, ran up the front steps, and fumbled in her purse for her keys. Anything with Adam seemed possible. They lived a life on the edge of disaster disguised by a quiet domesticity, a certain predictability in Adam's habits of living.

"Adam," Annie called.

There was no answer.

"Adam?"

"What do you think, Mama?" Alexandra asked.

"I think he probably turned on the lights and is upstairs working," Annie said, but she was not convinced.

The kitchen was in shambles. Brunnhilde sat on the table dipping her yellow paw into the open carton of milk. There were dishes broken on the floor; the trashbasket had been turned over, garbage and coffee grounds scattered. Siegy, Brunnhilde's kitten, was on the bottom shelf of the open refrigerator licking a bowl of tuna salad for the children's lunches, and on the floor beside the refrigerator a bottle of Ocean Spray Cranapple lay broken in a pool of red juice.

Nicholas climbed on a stool. "I think Papa came down to make dinner and lost his temper," he said.

"But he only comes downstairs in the morning," Alexandra said. "Never at night."

Annie took Siegy out of the refrigerator and closed the door, lifted Brunnhilde off the kitchen table, and poured out the rest of the milk. She picked up the glass on the floor beside the refrigerator and wiped up the juice.

"I think Nicholas is right," Annie said washing the kitchen table. She put the latch on the back door and turned off the lights downstairs except the one on the front porch.

. . .

Adam was sitting up in their bed, still in a robe, reading.

"Oh hello, Delirious," he said with a small wave. "I thought I heard someone come in but I assumed it was an addicted teenager looking for electronic equipment."

"Why didn't you answer me when I called?" Annie said, her voice unnaturally quiet. His nerves, he said, could tolerate only a small range of sound. "I was surprised about all of the lights and the kitchen."

"I like to keep your life full of surprises, my darling," Adam said.

Annie did not respond. She took her nightclothes out of the closet, kissed the children good night, and went into the bathroom.

In the mirror she examined her face, a small face with high cheekbones and wide-set brown eyes. She looked at her profile, reproducing the angle at which the priest on the subway had seen her, and from the side she was pleased with the way she looked. Adam had always said, "Keep your head turned, Annie. It may be uncomfortable but your profile is your best asset."

The overhead light was off in the bedroom when she went in and she climbed into her side of the bed.

"Your sister Athalia called to say that your sister Sylvie is eligible for parole."

"You spoke with her."

"I listened to her message on the machine. She says her cancer is worse and do you plan to come to Texas for Christmas?"

Annie pulled the sheet up under her chin.

"Do you plan to go to Texas for Christmas?"

"I don't know," Annie said.

"Yes or no."

"No," Annie said. "I don't think so."

"I hate Texas," Adam said.

"I know you hate Texas," Annie replied.

"I'll never go back there," he said turning off the reading light on his side of the bed.

He had not gone to Brammel with Annie when Ace died or two years ago when Rebecca was killed by a taxicab. When Annie took the children to see her family there, he went to see his parents in Connecticut.

"I should ask about the performance," he said turning on his side toward her.

"The performance was fine," Annie said.

"Outstanding?"

"No, not outstanding, but better than I had thought it would be." She hesitated. "My voice was very clear."

Clear—that was what musicians liked about her voice —the sweet clarity of it. But tonight, something had snapped when she began to sing, as if the instrument of voice itself had broken free and there was no limit to what she could do. She could sing like an angel. She could fly out from between the sheets where she was lying, away, away, away from Adam Blakemore, out the window, over the trees, to Ireland.

Now she lay quietly, planning tomorrow, waiting for Adam's breathing to deepen to sleep so she could slip out of bed and creep up the stairs to the attic where she kept her costume trunk.

It was a high trunk with wood slats and a rounded top and it held the one hundred and thirty-five changes of costume Annie had collected since she was nine years old and to which she still escaped as she had as a child in Brammel, standing on the edge of the bathtub so she could see herself in the mirror of the medicine cabinet on evenings when her sisters and brothers were out on dates, Ace out drinking, Rebecca in bed with Bible stories playing on the radio.

Russian was the heritage she had chosen for herself at eighteen when she read in *Parade* magazine that Leo Tolstoy had many descendants in America since the Bolshevik Revolution. Annie decided she'd be one of those. In college she dropped Dolores, called herself Anna Tolstoy Grainey, and started to wear hats.

At Northwestern, Annie wore a black felt cloche as protection from the fierce Chicago winds, and she discovered that in a hat she was a stranger, invisible, safe from scrutiny in her own corner of the world. She could go anyplace.

Now she tried on a black beret tilted like a Frenchman's, a broad-brimmed chocolate-colored felt hat, a dark straw hat with yellow grosgrain ribbon, a soft periwinkle blue hat with a rolled brim. She settled on the chocolate brown hat which, pulled down on her brow, cast her face in shadow. She would wear it tomorrow with a tweed straight skirt, ankle length, and a lightweight turtleneck sweater if the autumn weather continued to be humid.

"Annie?" Adam called.

She turned out the attic light, hurried softly downstairs, tiptoed across the bedroom, and slipped between the sheets.

"I was in the bathroom," she said.

"I didn't hear the water," Adam said. "I thought I heard you in the attic."

"No. I wasn't in the attic."

"I heard you there," he said.

Annie turned on her side, her back to Adam, and lay with the picture of the priest from the subway on her inside lids, brushing her lips softly with her fingers like kissing.

Much later, almost dawn, she woke to darkness and with a terrible start. The room was too hot and she had a sense of suffocating. When she had dragged herself from a deep sleep, she realized she was lying on her back and Adam's large hands were on her throat.

"I told you about the snoring, Delirious," he said in an even voice.

She pushed his hands away and got out of bed.

"If that was supposed to be funny," she said, "it wasn't."

"I'm glad for that," Adam said. "It wasn't supposed to be entirely funny."

Downstairs, she made a milk shake and sat wide awake in the dark on the living room couch with Brunnhilde on her belly.

"Delirious?" Adam called.

She didn't answer. She could hear him. It sounded as if he was moving around the bedroom but he didn't call again.

"I don't like your husband, Dolores," Ace had said to her just this past summer in the hospital in Dallas before he died.

"You don't know him, Papa," she had said. "You haven't seen him since the accident and he wasn't my husband then."

"I don't need to know him not to like him," Ace said. "He's not a nice man. He wasn't a nice man before the accident either."

"He was. He was a funny, sweet man," Annie said.

Her sister Clementine had been there and Richie, the second boy. They'd sat around the hospital room most of the afternoon without much conversation, watching the day fall in the window, and just before Annie got up to leave, Ace opened his eyes and looked at her.

"Just take the children and move to Maine," he'd said.

"Maine?"

"I read in a magazine there aren't any Baptists in Maine," he'd said in his crazy way.

"Are you thinking of leaving Adam?" Clementine asked later that evening when they were back at her house making supper.

"Of course not," Annie said. "I don't know what Papa was talking about."

"Alexandra told him Adam hit you twice—once across the face," Clementine said.

"Well, he didn't," Annie said. "He's never hit me."

"Children don't lie," Clementine said. "That's not like Alexandra."

Annie hesitated. "Maybe not," she said. "But I give you God's honest truth, Clem, he's never hit me once."

On the plane back to Washington after Ace had died, Annie asked Alexandra about the hitting.

"Why did you say that Papa has hit me when he hasn't, Lexa?"

"Because he might hit you," Alexandra said without looking up from her book.

. . .

That was in June when Ace died. In August they had gone to Connecticut to visit Adam's parents and since that visit Annie knew that Alexandra was right.

She did not go back upstairs. From time to time, she dozed and fell to dreaming but mostly she waited for the first light of dawn. At seven, she called school to say that she would not be in today because of the flu. Probably not tomorrow either. She made coffee, opened a frozen orange juice and mixed it, called Sara Ponder to babysit that night. Then she went upstairs to wake the children.

Adam was compulsive about time. At seven-thirty he had breakfast which Annie brought up to him, and he ate sitting in the chair by the bedroom window. Then he took a bath and just after the children left Annie helped him downstairs. This morning Annie worked quickly, bringing in the trashcans, feeding the cats, making breakfast, walking with the children to the corner of Fessenden and 38th where they met their friends, and by the time she was back in the house Adam was ready to be moved downstairs.

"I wasn't strangling you last night," Adam said. "If I wanted to strangle you, I would do it more efficiently."

"I hope you don't want to," Annie said trying to sound lighthearted. "Good-bye," she called.

"Annie?"

"I'm late, Adam," she said. "I'll call from school."

"It was a joke," he called.

She shut the front door, locked it, and hurried up the street to the Tenleytown Metro and onto the Red Line train to Silver Spring.

At Dupont Circle, she got out and walked down R Street arriving just across the street from Lacey's Guest House at ten minutes after eight.

5

Will Huston slept fitfully, waking just after seven with a plan forming.

It was a bleak, stormy day, the twentieth of November, and warm. The air coming through the open window was thick as pudding and he felt heavy-headed from it—almost ill.

He wrapped a towel around his waist, took his traveling articles kit, and opened the door. Across from his room another priest, dressed in a suit, his collar askew, stood in the open door of his room.

"The shower's in use," he said.

"You're waiting?"

"You go. I'm not in a hurry," the priest said indicating with some amusement the towel wrapped around Will's waist.

"Never mind," Will said. "I have plenty of time." Which was not entirely true. It was seven-fifteen and he wanted to be in front of Michael Maguire's house in an hour.

He wondered should he not have left his room in a towel. Perhaps priests were always fully dressed. He could not remember from his days at Trinity College or before whether he had ever seen a priest undressed or in a towel. He doubted it.

"You must be Irish," said the priest, a middle-aged man, florid, with enormous white eyebrows and a strained, unhappy look about his eyes quite uncommon in priests Will had known, even in Belfast, protected as they were by the conditions of their lives, their sense of certainty, their faith.

"Yes, Dublin." Perhaps that would explain the towel. In Dublin, priests appear in towels. That sort of thing.

"I'm from Minneapolis," the priest, who introduced himself as John Holloman, said. "I have cousins in County Cork but I've never been there myself."

"Nor I," Will said. Which was true. He'd been to Dublin, Belfast, and in between but that was it for the country of his fathers.

The door to the bathroom opened and a small sparrowlike elderly priest came out, smiled at Father John Holloman, gave Will a wave, and went into bedroom number 9 next door to Will's.

"Father Antonio lives here all the time," Father John explained. "You go on. I really have no plans until noon. I'll see you at breakfast."

In the bathroom, Will turned on the shower. He was nervous. His heart was racing and the steam from the hot water made him claustrophobic.

He took off his wig, stood under the shower and washed his hair, shaved, and went over the plan, which was to talk to Mrs. Michael Maguire.

Will Huston was gifted with women.

"Initially," his sister Bernadette said. "Until they get to know what a hard heart you are."

He had a capacity for intimacy, an ease which gave a woman, her defenses unalarmed, the sense of making love. And he was a man with an obsession; women fell in love with him for that, believing the power of his feelings about Jamey's death, the origin of his passion, was themselves.

He had had one wife in a marriage annulled after a year, and several women, two of whom he'd lived with—Maeve for two years, who bore him a stillborn daughter, and Maud, his co-lead in many Abbey productions, with whom he had lived for seven years mostly as a friend.

.   .   .

Will dressed, put on his wig, wiped the foggy mirror over the sink, and checked his appearance, which seemed to him to be that of a genteel middle-aged priest, and he was pleased. He went back to his bedroom and shut the door.

The plan he had in mind for Mrs. Michael Maguire had come to him in the middle of the night.

He had, he decided, only one mission in Washington. He wanted to sit someplace with Michael Maguire, a place from which the killer could not escape, had no reason to escape initially because he believed Will was Father James Grady, a man of God, a benevolent servant, a man to be trusted. And then, having won his trust, Will would lean forward in his chair. "I am not Father Grady," he'd say commanding Michael Maguire's attention, "I am Will Huston—remember me? Remember your friend, my cousin Brendan Mallory? Remember the boy you killed on the afternoon of July thirteenth, 1969, my brother, James Huston?"

He would persuade Mrs. Michael Maguire to arrange for a meeting between them. Although he did not know how he planned to engage her, he had never had difficulty persuading women.

There was a knock on the door. Will checked his watch. Seven forty-five. If he wanted to arrive at the Maguire house on Reservoir Road before Mrs. Maguire left and after Michael Maguire, he ought to be there soon to watch the house.

"Father?"

Will opened the door. Father John Holloman was standing at the doorway.

"Father," he said in a voice full of apology, "do you hear confessions?"

Will felt the blood run out of him. He did not even remember the last time he'd been to confession or the language or the prayers or the way the priest behaved—only his hot putrid breath coming through the little hole in the confession box.

"Of course," he said.

He opened the door and Father John came in.

Will stood—not certain what else to do—but imagining himself onstage as a priest, he thought it appropriate to stand and for the other priest to kneel, which Father John did, in front of him, his head down, his hands folded.

"It is easier for me to speak to you because you're a stranger from another country," he said. "Forgive me, Father, for I have sinned, it has been two months since my last confession and I have fallen in love." The story he told which went on and on—eight-ten, eight-fifteen, eight-nineteen—was about a love affair. Eighteen months ago, he said, he had fallen in love with a young woman, a girl really, a schoolgirl at Georgetown University, and he was following her. He couldn't help himself. He could no longer pray.

"Thank you, Father," the priest said after Will muttered an improvised absolution.

"Of course," Will said gathering up a few things to leave his room.

"You know, you feel familiar to me. Not familiar as a priest, but somehow I have a sense of knowing you."

"I'm just a small parish priest visiting my cousins in Silver Spring," Will said. "I don't get about much."

At the door, Father John stopped. "Did you ever love a woman before seminary?"

"Not before or after," Will said and shut the door behind him. "Good morning." He nodded and went down the stairs to the small parlor asking the receptionist if a taxi would be available outside.

"Up the street, on Connecticut Avenue," she said.

Outside the fog was beginning to lift but the heat was heavy for late autumn and the air tasted of pollution.

At any other time, he would have been happy to hear the confession of Father John. He loved the complicated lives of other people, the complexity without a personal cost. That was the pleasure in acting. Onstage, he could have a love affair. Onstage, he could die for Maud O'Connor's pure sweet love.

He saw a taxi and waved. As he was getting in, he noticed a young woman just beyond, in a long skirt and a broad-brimmed hat. She was waving for a taxi.

"Do you mind if I take another fare, Father?" the driver asked. "There's a woman signaling."

"I do mind," Will said sternly, settling in the back seat. "The corner of 35th Street and Reservoir Road, please."

6

At first Annie ran after the taxicab, lifting her long skirt, slipping on the mossy brick sidewalks wet with the morning rain, keeping the taxi with the priest in sight. At Florida Avenue, she hailed a Yellow cab and scrambled into the backseat.

"If you please," she said assuming an accent which sounded Slavic. "Follow the Diamond taxi." She wiped the perspiration off her forehead.

"Where're you going?" the driver, himself not American, perhaps Middle Eastern, asked her.

"I am following that taxi," Annie said. "It has a passenger who used to be my husband, you see." She felt she needed an excuse to follow another taxi.

"I don't want trouble," the driver said crossly. "You have too much trouble when you drive a cab."

The Diamond taxi turned right on Massachusetts Avenue.

"There will be no trouble from me," Annie said.

"You have money?"

"Of course I have money," she said.

"I've had trouble before," the taxi driver said. "One time at Union Station, the fare I picked up had a gun."

Annie laughed, a low throaty laugh, what she imagined would be the deep sorrowful laughter of a contemporary Russian woman.

"I have no gun," she said. "I have only a broken heart."

"And the man we're following? He doesn't have a gun?"

"I'm certain he doesn't," Annie said.

The Diamond taxi turned left on Wisconsin Avenue toward Georgetown.

"You saw him turn?" she asked.

"I'll follow him as long as we don't cross a bridge into Virginia," he said. "I don't go to Virginia."

At Reservoir Road, they turned left. The Diamond cab was a block ahead when they turned and Annie saw it stop.

"Here," she said.

"You want to get out here?"

"I'll wait to see what happens," Annie said. "Whether he gets out."

The taxicab stopped in the next block and the priest went around to the driver's side.

"Now I'll get out," Annie said. "Thank you very much."

The driver was a small-featured, dark-skinned man whose black eyes fixed on her with a familiar expression— sardonic, she thought, recognizing in the face of the taxi driver Ace, her father, the infidel.

"Three dollars fifty," he said. "Plus ten percent for the danger of the trip in case he had a gun."

She handed him five dollars.

"Maybe you can fix your broken heart today." He smiled, his thin lips forming a long brown line across white teeth. "Czech?" he asked.

"No, Russian," she said.

The priest was nowhere in sight. She ran up Reservoir Road, crossing 35th. Just beyond 35th Street, on the left, in one of the narrow brick houses, she saw him at the front door talking to a woman.

The house into which the priest quickly disappeared was indistinguishable from the other houses on the block except for the mass of dying white petunias spilling from window boxes on either side of the front door. She walked up the street, four houses beyond, and settled on the bottom steps of a similar house with a FOR SALE sign in the front yard. It was a gray day with a fine mist, no longer any rain but an intolerable thickness in the air, and she wished she had brought something to drink in her canvas bag—or something to read besides the libretto for *Don Giovanni,* which she opened. It was nine-ten by her watch. The sky was beginning to lighten and her stomach was rumbling from hunger and excitement. This was not the first time Annie Blakemore had followed a priest.

Annie knew she was different from the rest of the Graineys and somehow she thought that difference had to do with God. Or as Ace would say, "High hopes. You got high hopes, dum dum de dum dum de dum." And he'd do a little tap dance across the linoleum floor.

Rebecca Grainey's God covered their lives. He was a practical, judgmental, narrow-minded God whose order reduced the imagination to a world without mystery. In His orbit, the Grainey family lived day to day, poor, good-humored, dedicated to keeping their lives in careful order, to helping others, but they lived without great expectations.

And Annie had been born with great expectations.

"Don't you have daydreams?" she'd asked Clementine when they were small. "Like being famous?"

"I'm not going to be famous," Clementine said. "So why should I dream about it?"

"Because if you dream about it, then you could be," Annie said.

"I don't want to be famous, Dolores Ann. All I want

56.

is to have a house that's not a boarding house with enough money for curtains in the window.''

"I'd like curtains, too," Annie said. "But that's not enough."

"You've got too many plans to be a true Grainey," Clementine said. Which was true.

But Annie loved her family in spite of the fact that she knew she was going to fly—leave Texas, leave the Baptist church and the tiny circumference of their lives. And because she loved them, the urgency to leave made her a betrayer in her own heart, even now, her parents dead, Athalia sick with cancer, Sylvie in jail.

Besides, God had not entirely passed her by.

The first priest Annie had followed—and there had been three—was Father Anthony of the Church of the Annunciation at the end of Hunt Avenue in Brammel the spring Annie was thirteen and the real world had lost its mystery for her. Her girlfriends had crushes, her sisters had secret lives in the backseats of the cars in which they drove with slick-haired boys in tight jeans, her brothers smoked cigarettes in the laundry room of the boarding house where they lived. Such mysteries. Nothing was sufficient to her yearning until she slipped through the door of the Church of the Annunciation one Thursday before choir practice at First Baptist, knocked on the door of Father Anthony's office, and told him she wanted to be a Catholic.

"A secret Catholic," she said to him, her hands

folded in her lap, numbed at the sight of his thin, beautiful face.

"A secret Catholic?" he asked.

"We are Baptists except Papa who's nothing," she said. "So in my family it's a sin to be a Catholic. Like murder or," she said taking a dangerous leap, "like sex."

Afternoons, she went to private classes with Father Anthony, sequestered in the dark study smelling of damp cotton, warmed by his melodious voice. By the summer of her eighth grade year, she had completed her study for confirmation.

"But I can't be confirmed," she told Father Anthony. "I would die of it," she said.

"You wouldn't die of it, Dolores Ann," he told her.

"I would," she said.

Once he touched her on the cheek.

It was almost ten-thirty by her watch when Annie saw the front door across the street open and the priest go down the first flight of steps with a round-faced curly-haired woman of indiscriminate age. They shook hands and the priest walked down the second flight of steps, turned up the hill toward Wisconsin Avenue, walking slowly with a slight hesitation to his gait, perhaps a limp.

7

Mrs. Michael Maguire answered the door, a small woman with a clear, pleasant face and water-blue eyes set close to a fine straight nose. She was neatly dressed in garden colors in the way Englishwomen dress, a periwinkle wool suit and flowered blouse, not unattractive, agreeable, appropriate for the wife of the second secretary.

"Hello, Mrs. Maguire?" Will said, almost secure in the lines he had rehearsed in his mind all morning. "I'm Father James Grady from Dublin. Is Michael at home?"

"No, I'm sorry he's not." She was hesitant but stood aside, opening the door wider for Will to step in to the rush of stale air in the vestibule.

"You look familiar, but I doubt we've met." He

smiled and his voice was gentle with a lilt, not Irish exactly, softer, less accentuated. He made a habit of voices—even when he was young in grammar school with his cousin Brendan he would try voices, changing from week to week. Not to be mischievous exactly, although there was that of course, but for the sound of his voice in his ear, the language like music.

"I haven't seen Michael for a very long time," Will said. "But we were good friends in Belfast growing up. When I learned I was coming to America last week for an ecumenical conference in Washington, I got his address from a mutual friend."

"Yes?" she said with a kind of quizzical certainty familiar to him in British women.

"And here I am," he said with disarming openness. "You're English," he said. "You have a querying disposition, I suspect. So deceptive, Englishwomen." He laughed softly.

She shrugged but she was not going to ask him to leave, he could tell, not immediately. She was not uninterested in his arrival.

"I didn't know Michael until after he left Belfast," Mrs. Maguire said. "Did you go to school together?"

"No, I went to the Catholic school," Will said. "What we did together was drink."

"Drink?"

"I'm sure he doesn't drink now. But then he was quite a drinker. We both were."

She raised her eyebrows. "I met Michael in London after his parents died. You knew his parents?"

"I knew them," Will said, as he had of course read in the Belfast paper: "Esmé and Peter Maguire, now deceased. . . ."

"He seldom goes back to Belfast," she said. "Would you like coffee?"

"That would be lovely." Will followed her, pleased with the way things were going, uncertain how exactly to proceed, how much of a story to tell, how close to the truth to keep.

She poured a cup of coffee, indicating a chair for Will at the kitchen table. "Cream? Sugar?" she asked and sat down, cupping her chin in her hands in a way he would have thought provocative if there were not such a dowdiness about her.

"I was a solicitor when we met in London," she said. "And divorced with a small daughter now grown up. We met at a dinner of friends." She laughed lightly.

"I met Michael when I was seventeen in Belfast," Will said. "We used to go to Jack the Ripper's Pub after school and get quite saucy before we went home for tea." That had been true, although the dates were wrong. He had met Michael Maguire at Jack the Ripper's, where his cousin Brendan took him when he went over to the Mallorys' for supper, but that was after Will was in university and their meetings only went on in May and June of 1969.

"Michael never speaks about his life in Belfast except

his early life as a boy and then with a sparing of detail.''

The phone rang and she told the caller that yes, of course she'd be at coffee but a little late.

"I am not fond of the obligations of a secretary's wife," she said, talking softly as he had been to her, conspiratorial as if they were exchanging secrets. "Coffees, that sort of thing." She leaned across the table. "I am Priscilla Maguire."

He took her hand, just the fingers of her right hand, rubbed his thumb across the top in a gesture that would have been thought inappropriate were he not a priest. And in such spirit of safety, Priscilla Maguire responded, touching his arm, asking did he want a biscuit or a scone—strawberry and slightly stale.

"What was Michael like?" she asked, more interested in conversation than Will could have possibly hoped in his imaginings of this meeting.

"He was a terrible and ruthless man," Will thought to say. "A murderer." But he tried to remember Michael Maguire specifically from the few times they had met at Jack the Ripper's. Michael would have said that they were friends; that was the kind of man Will remembered—expansive, indiscriminate in his friendships. They were the only two university students among the young men who surrounded Brendan Mallory—the others, like Brendan, were more boisterous, philandering, high-drinking workers, carpenters, electricians. So he and Michael had something in common, including their attraction to Brendan, who was extroverted, given to street fighting and trouble. In the year Will finished Trinity, before the civil war broke out again in Belfast, when loyalists like Michael Maguire could still keep company with Catholics, Will and Michael got drunk together on a few occasions. Will could not remember whether he had liked Michael Maguire before the afternoon of July 13, 1969, although he doubted that he had.

"Michael was very cheerful and outgoing, a pleasant, intelligent man," Will said. "I liked him very much." The words fell easily for him.

"He is no longer so cheerful," Mrs. Maguire said. Priscilla Maguire, Will's friend Priscilla.

Sitting in the slick, steel-gray kitchen, the light falling across Priscilla Maguire's porcelain face, Will felt his heart pounding in his mouth. He had the sudden and familiar feeling of fear and excitement that he used to have as a boy standing on the high bridge over the River Lagan looking into the black, black water, knowing he could not chicken out; he was going to jump. He did not know where this small domestic meeting would take him—to what confrontation, to what action. And would this stirring of the black waters in his own soul lead to violence which he knew lay just below the surface of his rational mind?

.   .   .

The second telephone call was from Michael Maguire, whom Priscilla agreed to meet at the British embassy at six. She did not mention Father James Grady.

"I'll tell Michael you're here tonight," she said. "Father James Grady. That is how he'll remember you?"

"As James Grady," Will said. "Jamey." He wondered if the name Jamey would stir Michael's memory, make him suspicious, unwilling to meet with Will.

Mrs. Maguire put the cups in the dishwasher, the milk back in the fridge.

"So you were not a priest when you knew Michael?"

She followed him through the corridor, past the living room, which was not, as he had dreamed it, formal and English, but rather spare, beige, modern, with only an occasional pale print hanging on the white walls.

"I was a student," Will said.

"Like Michael," she said. "And why did you become a priest?" she asked. "I've always wondered that about priests—why, especially when one has been to university and had a life centered on doubt?"

"I became a priest to learn forgiveness," Michael said without hesitation, as if he had been thinking of the reasons for his conversion in case he was asked.

She laughed. "And did you learn forgiveness?"

Will took her hand, gave a small formal bow.

"I am sorry to say I did not," he said to her. "Forgiveness turns out to be a difficult subject for a man of my nature."

They shook hands and she handed him a card.

"It has our telephone number at home and Michael's at work, so please call to make arrangements. Or just stop by tomorrow evening, about six might be good. Michael will be home, I'm certain, and I'll be here shortly after six-thirty." She waved. "I'll tell Michael that Jamey Grady will be by for drinks at six."

Will walked slowly up Reservoir Road, suddenly weary, worse than weary—ill. He hesitated at the corner and leaned against a STOP sign. His arms were heavy and his chest tight. Perhaps, he was not certain—he tried to calm himself—there were pains in his chest. And what an odd turn of events that would be to have a heart attack. He was always having heart attacks, he reminded himself—but a real heart attack had never actually developed. "Hyperventilation," the doctor called it. But this time, the event would be real. He saw himself in intensive care at the nearby hospital. Father James Grady. And who was next of kin? they'd ask him. No kin, he would say. Friends or other priests with whom the attending doctor could be in touch? Only Priscilla Maguire, he'd have to tell them—and of course his drinking companion from Belfast, Michael Maguire, second secretary of the British embassy, wanted for murder.

8

Will was seventeen when Jamey was born—an angel of God, his mother called this late, unexpected baby, the ninth child, second son of Maureen and Thomas Huston, whose family had been in Northern Ireland, now Ulster, forever. They remained as most of the Catholic families had done after the Government of Ireland Act of 1920, divided the country between the Irish Free State in the south and Ulster in the north, six counties represented by twelve MPs in the British Parliament. Tom Huston owned Mailbones Pub in downtown Belfast where he lived quite comfortably in the rooms above the pub with his nine children, Will at the top—brooding, impetuous Will Huston, considered gifted amongst the ordinary young men of St. John's parish, the only man to go off to Trinity College and read law. Then seven girls—Kathleen, Beatrice, Bernadette, Mary, Maeve, Nell, Molly—and Jamey, young enough to be Will's own son.

It was a wonder to Will to have a brother. He had found himself obsessed by the oddness as well as the familiarity of a miniature boy sleeping in a basket in his room. At seventeen, self-conscious, ambitious, overtaken with the importance of his own life, and no believer in miracles, Will fell in love with the baby.

"You've gone soft, Will," his sister Beatrice said watching Will lean over the basket to play with the baby's fingers and toes. "It's disgusting."

"Yeah, yeah," Will said. But nothing stopped him. It was his last year in school before university but he came home after football and took the baby strolling down Aiken Street. Weekends, when he ought to have been studying for the A levels, he took Jamey with him to football matches or to the movie house or to parties with his friends. He found himself pretending to be Jamey's father.

"You'll have your own chance, you know, Will. You could have as many sons as I've had daughters," Tom Huston said one night closing up at Mailbones Pub.

Will shrugged. "I've taken leave of my senses, going soft on babies," he said.

"Jamey is just like you, unspoiled by experience," his sister Nell, his favorite sister, said. "He's even got a cleft."

"Maybe that's it," Will said lying on his cot with Jamey sleeping on his chest. "Or maybe I'm a born father."

Will knew he wanted to teach Jamey Huston what he had learned before his brother's life became the one Tom and Maureen Huston and his sisters lived. The Hustons were good people, generous and with open hearts, but their lives contracted year by year, fixed in place by the narrow parameter of Mailbones Pub and the shops on Arch Street and St. John's Roman Catholic Church. They had no dangerous thoughts. No dreams.

There was an uneasiness in Ulster in 1969. The Irish Catholics, in the spirit of the civil rights marches in America, organized a seventy-mile march from Belfast to Londonderry to protest an inequitable voting system which reflected the Protestant majority; they protested discrimination in jobs and in housing as well. At Burn Tollet Bridge they were ambushed and beaten by a Protestant mob.

Will had just graduated with high honors from Trinity College, with a future in law. Although he was a sympathizer with his own people, there was no reason for him to be involved. He thought of himself as a Dubliner, no longer a citizen of Belfast. But he was home that summer helping his father in the pub and his mother, who'd had a hysterectomy, spending one last summer season with his family, with his cousin Brendan who had plans to move to America in the fall, and especially with Jamey.

The thirteenth of July 1969 was a bright, sunny Sunday afternoon in the north of Ireland, not a day for trouble. When Will set out with Jamey for Sunday dinner with the Mallorys west of Falls Road, he did not know that earlier in the day the Catholics on Falls Road had had clashes with the police. In fact, when he turned the corner to the street of mud-brown row houses where his cousins lived and saw a crowd of people down the road beyond the Mallorys' cottage, he thought there must be a party, the weather was so fine.

He stopped his car across the street from the Mallorys' and got out, crossing around the front of the car to let Jamey out of the front seat. Usually, he would have hoisted Jamey up on his shoulder and later, thinking back to the exact details of that afternoon, he wondered why he had not. Just hoisted him up on his shoulder and marched triumphantly as he often did onto the Mallorys' front stoop with his charge who looked very much like Will had looked at Jamey's age, with black hair in square bangs and cheeks flushed red with the damp weather—a beautiful boy, sunnier than Will had been, innocent of trouble, protected by a rank of siblings. Instead, Will had taken Jamey's hand and crossed the street toward the cottage where Brendan was standing on the front steps, smoking a cigarette.

"Hey Bren," Will had called.

He did remember later that Brendan held up his hand for silence and did not turn his attention away from the activity at the end of the block. Other people were looking as well, leaning out of their windows, standing on their steps, in the shadow of their front doors.

Perhaps if Will had been less preoccupied with thoughts of grandness—Will Huston, MP, Will Huston, Barrister, Will Huston, High Honors, Trinity College, Dublin—thoughts like that—he would have noticed that the spirit in the air was unsettled, that the gathering down the street was hostile.

What he did remember was someone up the street from the Mallorys' shouting *"Watch out!"* He saw a look of terror cross Brendan's face—and he saw, too late, that the crowd was headed toward him with Michael Maguire in the lead.

"Get in your houses," Michael was shouting. "Get in your houses or you'll be shot."

But Michael Maguire didn't wait. He fired the first shot as he was speaking.

Will had just leaned down to lift Jamey up in his arms, to run with him to the Mallorys', when Michael fired another shot and Jamey slipped from Will's arms to the ground.

What happened after that Will remembered in pieces and with the help of Brendan. He picked Jamey up and ran into the house—laying him, still breathing, on the couch in the arms of his aunt, Brendan's mother. Then he ran outside after the crowd of loyalists, after Michael Maguire, running as fast as he could although his legs were leaden and he could not breathe.

Someone—Brendan did not remember who it was—but a man from a house up the street from Brendan's tackled Will and brought him to the ground. "You're going to be killed," he said. "That crowd of murderers will kill you."

"I don't care," Will said as Brendan led him back to the house where his aunt had covered Jamey with a blanket. "Let them kill me," he said. "They are welcome to kill me as soon as I kill Michael Maguire."

There were riots all day in Belfast. By nightfall, one hundred and seventy-five, both Catholics and loyalists, had been injured. Eleven people were dead, all Catholics shot by loyalists. And one Catholic child.

9

Annie walked on the other side of the street from the priest, crossed Wisconsin Avenue keeping sight of his robe through the traffic that separated them. He was walking very slowly, almost with a hesitation to his gait, and she wondered if he were suddenly unwell. At the crossing of S Street, he went into a small café and she dashed across Wisconsin Avenue, waiting for several moments outside the café, in case he had planned only to buy cigarettes or a cup of coffee to go.

When she did go inside, he was seated in a booth with the *Washington Post* opened on the table and a cigarette in his mouth. She went to the counter, ordered a lemonade with a lot of ice and a sugar donut, and sat on the edge of a stool.

Will was reading when a young woman in a broad-brimmed brown hat walked in the café. *Thomas Bradshow, photographer, died of AIDS at 34. Mary Hoser, Secretary at the Department of Transportation, died of injuries sustained when the car in which she was driving crossed the median strip on Route 50. Billy System, 61, retired accountant died of a heart attack in Coral Gables, Florida, where he was visiting his daughter.*

He was imagining: *Father James Grady, priest from Dublin, Ireland, died of a heart attack at the Rabelais Café in Georgetown. There are no known survivors.* And would the obituary of Michael Maguire be longer than Will's and attest to a life better lived? *Michael Maguire, Second Secretary of the British Embassy, age 41, was murdered in his bedroom on Reservoir Road by his childhood companion Father James Grady, alias William Huston of Dublin, Ireland, actor, playwright.*

"Father," Annie said standing beside the booth where he was sitting.

"Excuse me?" Will asked closing the Metro section, not wishing to be observed reading the obituaries, disturbed by the familiarity of this young woman.

"I'm so sorry to bother you," Annie said quickly, glad the café was dark; perhaps he would not recognize her from the subway. "I am in a terrible dilemma."

"I have an appointment, my child," Will said, although certainly she was not a child, a young woman of perhaps thirty-five with quite a pretty face, delicate features, high cheekbones, but ''child'' seemed the right thing to say to calm her so he could escape her dilemma and go about his solitary business.

''Please, Father,'' Annie said. ''It will only be a moment.''

Will hesitated. ''Is it a priest you need?''

Annie nodded, uncertain of what she would say to him.

''I am sorry, but I can't take care of you,'' he said. ''I am a priest from Dublin with an appointment in twenty minutes and a plane back to Ireland tomorrow. You should go to a church where you will find an American priest to help you.''

Will folded the newspaper under his arm and got up. ''I'm awfully sorry,'' he said turning his face away from hers.

It was almost eleven when Annie left the café just after the priest. On a public telephone on the street, she called the Washington Opera to see if she was supposed to perform again that night, but Marcia was well so she was simply expected at five for a rehearsal of *Don Giovanni* on which she worked during the short opera season with the stage manager. Then she called Adam.

''Where are you?'' he asked.

"At lunch break," Annie said.

"Where is lunch break, Delirious? You were not at work today."

Annie's breath stopped.

"I called and they said you had called in with the flu," Adam said.

"I did," Annie said evenly, unprepared for his discovery. "I called in sick because I need to practice for tonight, so I'm in a practice room at Levine."

"I don't believe you," Adam said.

"Of course that's what I'm doing," Annie said. "I'll be home by three."

She checked her watch. The priest was down the street about a block ahead of her, his hand out hailing a taxi.

She would go to the practice rooms at Levine School of Music where she studied voice and then she had to be home by the time the children arrived. Especially now that Adam had discovered her deception.

She walked to Levine at 36th and T Streets, went into the ladies' room to wash her face. Perhaps she should send the children to Clementine, she thought. Soon. Maybe tomorrow. If Adam wanted to hurt her, if he was really crazy as he seemed more and more to be, losing his small hold on rationality, then he might hurt the children.

It was lunchtime in Texas and Clementine was at home having lunch with her son, Louey, now grown, a night waiter at a taco restaurant. Of course, she said when she heard Annie's concern. Send the children. I'll keep them as long as you like. Come yourself, she said.

"I'll think about it," Annie said. "I have to work. The opera is on for the next few weeks and there's always a chance I'll get to cover if someone is sick. But if Adam doesn't pull himself together soon, I will come."

"I doubt he's dangerous, Dolores Ann. Redheads never are," Clementine said brightly. "I saw a picture recently of Jesus in which his hair was red, but he didn't look so good with red hair."

"I don't know about red hair," Annie said. "I don't know about Adam either."

"Well, send them on to Texas for as long as you like," Clementine said.

"Thanks, Clem," Annie said. "Maybe tomorrow. I'll let you know." She hung up the telephone.

If the priest was telling the truth, not simply trying to get rid of her, then Annie had only one more day before he left for Ireland. Unless, of course, the children went to Clementine's house and Annie packed up, took a taxi to Dulles Airport, and followed him to Dublin.

The air was dead in the large practice room overlooking the parking lot of Levine School of Music and Annie's throat was too dry to sing. Instead she stood in front of the practice mirror to one side of the piano, stood very straight, her back arched just slightly, her head tilted to one side, and hummed the words to Donna Anna's aria in *Don Giovanni*.

"Dolores Ann's flighty," Athalia had said crossly to Rebecca when Annie was small. "The way she does her eyes."

"It's not proper to make people laugh the way you

do, Dolores Ann," Rebecca said. "Not Christian, making faces with your eyes."

"I don't do anything, Mama," Annie had said. "I just am what I am."

And there was an unplanned quality about Annie Blakemore, something accidental, unself-conscious, that pleased people to be in her presence. She gave a person confidence looking at the world without judgment as she did, with the eyes of a child.

"Nothing gets to you, does it, Dolores Ann?" Clementine had said to Annie that summer sitting on one of the turquoise plastic couches outside Ace's room waiting for him to die. "You've got a sick husband who thinks you're white trash and Mama hit by a taxi and Papa's gone from drunk to dead and Sylvie in jail, troubles to sink a ship, and here comes Dolores Ann cheerful as Christmas."

Gloomy Athalia suffering with her cancer shook her head. "Dolores Ann just doesn't have the same deep feelings some of us have got," she said. "She never went to church."

"I don't know about that, Athalia," Clementine said. "We might not understand Dolores Ann as well as you think."

Annie sunk into the plastic sofa, closed her eyes, put her hands over her ears, and made a face. Nothing changed. Here she was almost forty years old and they talked about her, right in front of her as if she were not English-speaking or were brain dead.

"Why don't you ask me about myself if you want to know?" Annie said.

"Because you wouldn't tell us," Clementine said. "You keep your troubles to yourself and I swear they must burn a hole in your heart."

Annie opened the window beside the piano. Outside the air was motionless with the rancid smell of car exhaust. She felt weak and anxious, perhaps from the heat, she thought, or the excitement of her priest. But as she stood at the window watching a young mother lift her son, clutching a tiny violin, out of his car seat, a familiar sense of rising panic made her mouth bone dry and she wanted to run out of her own skin.

Fixed on watching the child follow his mother across the parking lot, she was suddenly and unaccountably ill, as if the room were closing in on her.

The picture in her mind's eye was of Alexandra and Nicholas on the front porch of their house. Behind them Adam, walking without the aid of crutches, opened the front door.

"Why Nich-o," he said. "And Lexa. Come in."

"You're walking, Papa," Nicholas said.

"A miracle," Adam said. "It just happened while I was making your lunch. Now come in. I have your lunch ready. Chicken salad and cookies."

"Yum yum," Nich-o said, his fear of Adam melting.

"Watch not to let the squirrels in when you come."
Adam locked the door behind them.

He sat with them as they ate their sandwiches, talking
as if he had a new and pressing interest in their daily lives.
And then in the newsreel spinning through Annie's brain,
as they sat side by side licking the icing from their Oreo
cookies, Adam killed them. He strangled them—first Lexa,
then Nich-o—and carried their bodies to the living room,
stuffing them in the small box under the lid of the window
seat.

"Where are the children?" Annie asked a few minutes later when she arrived home. She put her backpack in
the hall, sat on the window seat over the bodies of her
children, talking to Adam.

"They've gone to heaven, darling Delirious," he said.
"They have learned from your religious family that heaven
is such a pleasant place to be."

Out of breath, Annie dialed home. It rang four times—of
course, Adam wouldn't answer—and then the sweet voice
of Alexandra. "This is the Blakemores, please leave a message at the beep."

"Adam," Annie said into the phone. "Adam, please
pick up."

It was one-fifteen on the clock over the telephone.
School had let out at noon for lunch and the children got
home by twelve-fifteen, Annie thought. She ran down the

back steps of Levine to 36th Street, hailed a taxi. In the backseat she sat in the middle so she could catch her reflection in the taxi's rearview mirror to see if she looked as ill as she felt, ill enough to die.

"Could you hurry?" she said to the driver. "It's an emergency."

"Drive careful," the driver said pleasantly in broken English. "No hurry, no ticket."

Adam was on the front porch as she dashed up the steps, sitting with a demeanor of surprising informality, his pale, lifeless legs propped on the railings. He was in woolen socks and a sweater. Except for the wheelchair, he looked almost normal, like the husbands of other women Annie knew, at ease with himself.

She ran up the steps.

"Are the children home?" she asked breathlessly. "Have they gone back to school?"

Adam put down his book. "It's only one-thirty. They haven't come home yet."

"What about lunch?" Annie said.

"Annie, you know they didn't come home for lunch," Adam said almost kindly.

Annie leaned against the porch railing out of breath.

"You made arrangements for them to eat at school just this week to protect them from my temper, remember? Although the excuse you gave was that the weather will be turning too cold for them to walk home." Adam's face took on a look of familiar exasperation. "You made them sandwiches yourself this morning after Siegfried ate the tuna fish last night."

"Oh brother," she said wiping the nervous perspiration from her forehead with the sleeve of her jacket. "I don't know what's the matter with me. They've always come home for lunch and I completely forgot that I changed the arrangement."

Adam closed his book.

"What is the matter with you, Annie?" he asked scrutinizing her.

"Nothing. I'm anxious," she said. "I feel like I'm going to have a panic attack."

"You need to see a doctor about these attacks," Adam said. "You are beginning to seem a bit crazy."

"I don't need to see a doctor." She folded her arms across her chest. "I was practicing and suddenly I was afraid something had happened to the children. That's normal, I'm a mother."

She opened the door, dumped her backpack in the hall, and went in the living room.

Brunnhilde lay in the shaft of sunlight on top of the window seat, and Annie, the nightmare picture of Nicholas and Alexandra stuffed in the space under the window seat still bold in her mind's eye, lifted the cat, moved the cushion, and picked up the lid. In the small wooden space there was a black banana peel, a lavender bandanna, a red ball, and the carcass of a small gray mouse. She closed the lid and sat down weak-kneed.

Since Adam's accident, Annie had had waking nightmares coming on her unexpectedly.

A picture of personal disaster would fly into her head, persist in its frame, carefully detailed, with the stubbornness of a migraine.

"Trauma does that," Clementine had said to Annie the week Ace died. They were sitting in her kitchen the day after the funeral, Clementine off work for the week. "After Mama was hit by the taxi, I'd start shaking out of nowhere, at the grocery store, picking up some bread at the market, at my computer at work. The doctor gave me some pills."

"The trouble is," Annie said, "I believe these nightmares are a sign."

"They are," Clementine said. "They're a sign you had a trauma, which you did, and your nerves are jumbled.

"I mean a sign of the future," Annie said solemnly.

"From God?" Clementine laughed and tousled Annie's hair. "Why, Dolores Ann! I didn't think you gave God the time of day. Mama would be pleased to hear the good news of your conversion."

"It's not about God I'm having nightmares, Clementine. I think it's about guilt."

"Don't let him bully you into thinking such trash," Clementine said putting out mint tea and cookies. "What happened to Adam was not your fault."

Annie put her feet up on Clementine's kitchen table, broke a cookie in half, and gave her sister, after careful examination, the larger piece.

"You weren't in the car with us, Clem, so you can't exactly say it wasn't my fault because you don't know."

In the kitchen, Annie poured a glass of cranberry juice. She took a pear which was ripening on the windowsill and sat down. The front door opened and Adam, banging his wheelchair into walls, came through the living room, into the dining room, and stopped at the kitchen door.

"Would you like a pear?" Annie asked. "Or something else?"

Adam pulled his wheelchair beside her. "Why did you call in sick to Ellington?" he asked lifting his right leg so it crossed with his left leg at the knee.

"I told you, Adam. I called you from Levine," Annie said.

"I don't believe you," Adam said. "Where have you been all day?"

"Where I said," Annie said wearily. She took another pear and put it on the table beside Adam. "Tea?" she asked out of habit but he didn't reply.

In the bathroom, she took off her long tweed skirt, her turtleneck, her slip, her bra, and stood in her panties, looking in the mirror at her face which appeared, to her surprise, to be her normal face, even after the drama of the last few hours.

It was not crazy to worry about what Adam would do to the children, she told herself, checking the way her hair looked straight back off her face like a boy's. She was not the one who was crazy.

II

"Dear Clemmie," Annie had written in the summer of 1978 from Williamstown, Massachusetts, where she and Adam were doing summer stock and living, disguised as lovers, over the delicatessen on Main Street, "I'm coming to Brammel with Adam Blakemore. He is the one I told you about from Northwestern with whom I'm living in a very nice apartment with curtains and window boxes. Tell Mama. We'll drive—he has his own car—and be in Texas probably the weekend of August 26, staying a week. Then I have to come back to go to the school I mentioned called Juilliard in New York City. They've given me enough money to go for free so it's crazy not to—if you'll sort of tell Mama, who thinks I'm coming back to Texas, that

Texas is just not the right place to be the kind of singer I want to be.

"Another thing. I'd like to stay with you and Manuel if Louey doesn't mind us having his room—since I can't see Adam and Ace and Mama having much to say to each other.

"To give you an idea, Adam lives in a house the size of the Baptist church, not brick but painted white wood with blue shutters, and they have a yard bigger than the Brammel Recreational Park. I stayed in a guest room with guest towels in the bathroom and soap in the shape of blue seashells and rose petals in silver bowls. Also they sit down for dinner with candles and somebody called Elsie waits tables and there's no mention at the table of God.

"You can sort of understand why I don't want to stay at Mama's.

"I'm really upset about Sylvie. There are plenty of drugs here in Williamstown too and some of the actors mess around. But I don't. You didn't say whether her boyfriend was the one held up or the one doing the holdup when he got killed.

"Love to you and Manuel and Louey and Sally Jane and the cats and the bird, D. Ann."

"Dear Dolores Ann," Clementine wrote back, "I didn't show your letter to Mama and Ace and certainly not to God's own daughter, Athalia. But the fact is, you've got too big for your britches. So watch yourself.

"Clementine. (I'm going by my full name since I turned thirty-five last year.)"

Annie had lain on the bed in Louey's room in late August 1978, after church, waiting for Adam to come back from the drugstore half a mile down the road. But he'd been gone two hours and she had a feeling in her stomach that he was gone for good.

Clementine looked in the bedroom. "Dolores Ann?" she said. "I'm making this lunch for everyone—Mama's coming with Billy Joe and she says Ace is sober enough to make it and even Sylvie—and you lying there like a cream puff princess."

"I feel sick," Annie said.

"Great." Clementine threw up her arms. "So we're having the big dinner where the whole family meets the boyfriend and you're sick."

"I don't think you like him very much, Clementine," Annie said.

"I've met worse," Clementine said.

"He's shy and his family is sort of proper."

"Stuck up," Clementine said. "He doesn't like us is the truth." She sat down on the edge of the bed. "I'm making roast beef and a chocolate cake with double chocolate icing. What does his mama serve at her table in her house like the Baptist church?"

Annie laughed in spite of herself.

"Chicken," Annie said. "Mostly chicken, never roast beef. And Adam's mama can't bake so there's no chocolate cake."

Clementine looked very pleased.

"Think of it," she said. "Papa's actually sober and he may wear one of Richie's suits."

Clementine had set the table with a purple flowered sheet and cloth napkins and place cards—Clementine, Manuel, Mama, Papa, Dolores Ann, Sylvie, Athalia, Big Bill, who was Athalia's poor husband, Richie, Billy Joe, Tom Boy.

"Place cards, Clem," Annie had said. "You're something else."

"I saw a picture of this table in a magazine at the checkout counter and I bought it and copied the picture."

Louey lay on the couch in the living room and watched suspiciously from under the bill of his baseball cap.

"So what's the big deal?" he asked Annie. "Are you getting married, Aunt Dolores?"

"Maybe," Annie said.

"To him?"

"Him called Adam," Annie said.

"The rooster. That's what Sally Jane calls him. Adam the Rooster." Louey pulled his baseball cap down. "I don't like family lunches. I like eating dinner in front of the TV."

"With your hands," Annie said. "Why don't you eat with a knife and fork today?"

Louey crossed his eyes.

"Mama?" he called.

"Uh-huh."

"Aunt Dolores says I don't eat right."

"She's correct. All sweets and no vegetables."

"No," Louey said. "She means proper. So I'm not coming to lunch."

"You certainly are coming to lunch. In decent clothes."

Adam was in the bedroom when Annie came in.

"That took you a long time," she said sitting down beside him. "I couldn't imagine what you were doing so long at the drugstore."

"I didn't go to the drugstore," Adam said.

"So where did you go then?" Annie asked, sensing even before he spoke that his response was not what she wanted to hear.

"I went into Dallas to buy a plane ticket to New York."

"To New York?"

"Home," Adam said.

"But what about the lunch, Adam? Clementine's cooking this lunch all by herself without anybody called Elsie in the kitchen and she's doing roast beef even though she hasn't got enough money for panty hose most weeks."

"I'm coming to lunch."

"And she's got flowers on the table."

"I said I was coming to lunch," Adam said. "My plane is at seven-thirty."

"Tonight?"

"Tonight."

"And you're going back for good?"

"I'm going back for now," he said.

In the mirror over Louey's bureau, Annie could see herself, her black hair framing her face like the face of an angel, she thought, above the sweetheart neckline of her pale yellow dress.

"What about your car?" She folded her arms across her chest. "Are you flying your car in the baggage compartment?"

"I'm giving you my car, Annie," Adam said in a voice weighted with sentiment. "For keeps."

"Why, that's very nice of you, Adam Blakemore," Annie said. "That's a very dear and sweet thing for you to do, pay me back for leaving me high and dry with that nice red car your Papa gave you for graduating from college. I want you to know how grateful I am for these years of your acquaintance." She took a glance at herself in the mirror to see if her looks had held during the last conversation.

Adam found her in the backyard lying on the hammock with a yellow cat stretched out on her belly.

"Don't say a word to me, Adolf Hitler," she said.

"Judas Iscariot. P. J. Caligula. Beat it. I'm going to throw up."

"I won't say anything, Annie. I just don't think we ought to ruin the party for Clementine."

"You are a man of real sensitivity to think of my sister like that."

He tried to sit on the hammock with her but she threw the cat in his direction.

"I just hope you won't make a scene," he said.

"Beat it," Annie said. "I'm saying prayers for your sudden death and I don't want to be interrupted."

At dinner, Sylvie kept a strange soft high-pitched sound going through the conversation, which was primarily Rebecca's and had to do with Adam's religious upbringing. Everyone in the family had married Baptists, so far, she said, except Clementine's husband, Manuel, was Roman Catholic but that was because he was Mexican. And all the boys had married Baptists but Sambo whose wife, Dale, had persuaded Sambo to convert to the Church of Jesus Christ of Latter-Day Saints, which allowed him the opportunity to convert his living and dead relatives to Mormonism without their permission and was the reason he hadn't been invited to this dinner at Clementine's. Adam said he was not a member of the Church of Jesus Christ of Latter-Day Saints or any other church for that matter and Annie said it was no one's business but she, for one, knew that Adam didn't believe in God or Jesus Christ or anyone else but a few dead dictators.

"He believes in many gods," Annie said. "The god of the Sun, of the Moon, of Cruelty to Animals, the god of Sin, the god of Hate, the god of Betrayal."

"Dolores Ann," Rebecca said.

"I had been under the impression that you two had come to Texas to tell us something," Ace said. He was dressed in Richie's suit which Richie wore to work as a driver at Plumley's Funeral Home.

"Well, in fact, we had," Adam began.

"Adam," Annie said in a stage whisper, dropping her head in her palm. "Don't above all say what you're about to say to my family."

"For chrissake, Annie. What do you think I'm about to say?"

"About God," Annie whispered.

"Dolores Ann, you are stirring up trouble," Rebecca said.

"So you just came here without any plans for marriage and stayed together in Louey's room." Ace's voice was rising.

"You're absolutely right, Papa," Annie said reaching across the narrow dining room table, touching her father's wrists. "Adam and I came to Texas with plans," she said. "And those plans have changed."

Clementine tried to keep up the conversation, talking about what a hot summer it had been and the trouble she'd had with her garden and the friend of hers at church who'd been diagnosed with MS and was cured by eating banana peels and how everyone said that Dolores Ann had the best voice there had ever been at First Baptist Brammel. Ace kept his eyes on Adam, and Rebecca, insensitive to the subtleties of human intercourse, told the story of her father's deathbed conversion. But by the time dessert came, a shiny black chocolate cake with real rose petals around the edges, the conversations had unwound and stretched the length of the long table like limp thread.

In the middle of dessert, Ace folded his arms across his chest. "It's almost four o'clock and I have promised my friend Mr. Avedon that I'd shoot some pool this afternoon with him. I thank you, Clementine, for the best dinner I have ever eaten in my life including Christmas." He reached over and shook Adam's hand. "I am glad to have made your acquaintance, Mr. Blakemore. I suppose we won't see each other again since I don't travel to Connecticut but I want to tell you," he said in a soft-spoken, matter-of-fact tone of voice, "I've been looking at you during lunch and can't help wondering whether it's common for people from your kind of family to have skin so thin you can see the blood running in the veins."

"And it's blue," Louey said.

"Everybody's blood is blue until the air turns it red, dummy," Sally Jane said.

"Sally Jane, please mind your manners," Clementine said halfheartedly.

"What was Ace talking about?" Rebecca asked. "Ace?" she called, but he was gone out the front door and down the road on foot to the firehouse.

"He's really going?" Clementine asked Annie.

Annie nodded, trying to hold on to her tears, but they came anyway in a fury down her flushed cheeks. "After all your troubles."

"Never mind. It was worth it to see Papa in a suit."

Annie stood at the door to Louey's room and watched Adam stuff his clothes in the suitcase. He called his mother in Connecticut to say he was coming back and would some-one meet his plane at La Guardia.

"So you're not getting married," Louey said.

"Doesn't look that way," Annie said.

"He's a creep anyway," Louey said.

Annie drove the red Toyota to Dallas, at Adam's sugges-tion. She did not realize the white heat of her rage until they were closed in the car together, Adam sitting beside her, his arms folded across his chest, staring at the long black line of hot asphalt which curved in front of them.

"You promised," she said as they pulled onto the Southwest Freeway.

"I said maybe we'd get married," he said wearily. "I never promised."

"You promised," Annie said fiercely. "You said you adored me." Her breath, tight in her chest, came in small windstorms. "You said you would love me forever. That you had never loved anyone but me."

"I haven't," Adam said. "That isn't the point."

"I told you my family was different and you said of course you would love them too." Annie pulled out in front of a gasoline truck, passing a blue Honda, a convertible with the top down in the terrible heat, pressing the gas pedal.

"We have lived in a cocoon, Annie. I didn't know that until I got here. We're too different. Everything about us," he said grabbing on to the dashboard. "Annie, slow down."

Her foot flattened on the accelerator past a white Corvette, an old green Chevrolet, a pickup truck, flying down the highway.

"Who did you think I was?" Annie asked. "Related to the queen of England? The daughter of a duke? You knew me. You knew me very well."

"You're an actress, Annie. I didn't know." His voice was quiet. "Will you please slow down? If I talk to you sweetly, if I explain everything, will you please drive carefully?"

"No," Annie shouted, screeching into a curve. "No. No. No."

"Please," Adam said. "We're both going to be killed."

"No we're not," Annie said pulling out to pass a long

truck. "I'm not going to be killed. I'm already dead," she said. And either she lost control of the car then or else she simply drove into the side of the blue delivery truck.

"Annie, turn your wheel!" Adam shouted as the red Toyota hit the side of the delivery truck, started to spin off the highway, over and over, landing on its side in a ravine. When the car had stopped rolling, Annie lifted up on her elbow and saw Adam lying against the window on the passenger side, his lips white and curled over his teeth.

When Will asked the taxi driver about guns, the young man with a ponytail braided with ribbons took him to a gun shop on Georgia Avenue in Silver Spring, a small shop located between a wholesale novelty store and a wig shop.

"I live in a dangerous neighborhood," Will said. "Just this weekend my friend Father Brendan was killed as he walked home with breakfast for his elderly mother."

"My God," the taxi driver said. "They will kill anyone. Even near Washington, the center of the world, it's got so bad they can kill a priest."

"That's true," Will said. "And I think about my poor mother. I am her only son—my father is dead. I owe it to her to protect myself from the fate of Father Brendan.''

"My mom's dead of drink," the taxi driver said matter-of-factly. "I didn't see her sober for ten years and then kaput. Last December eleventh. So," he said, pulling up in front of the gun shop, "have you ever had a gun?"

"Never," Will said sorting through his change for a tip. Which was true although he knew how to shoot. He had learned early, as a lot of Belfast boys had learned. "You have to think twice about a world where priests feel the need to carry guns."

"You think you could shoot it if you had to?" the driver asked, clearly pleased with the novelty of his fare.

Will shrugged. "I have found that mostly in life I am able to do the things I have to do," and as he said it, he knew that what he said was true.

"Well, I've shot a gun," the taxi driver said. "It made me feel like God." He smiled at Will, a curious half smile, and Will felt suddenly they had gone too far in their conversation. The driver was beginning to make implications.

"Thank you for your advice," Will said and shut the door.

"Good luck, Father," the taxi driver called.

Will waved and went into the shop.

GUNS: BOUGHT AND SOLD was painted in yellow and black

on the glass front of the gun shop, and a small bell rang when Will entered. A man was behind the counter, a middle-aged man with glasses, and he was small—small hands particularly like the hands of a woman, small lips and eyes set very close together against the high bridge of his nose. Will could tell he was a quiet man even before he spoke; the shop felt empty in spite of his presence at the counter and Will was uncomfortable.

"I'm looking for a handgun," he said. "A revolver."

The man folded his hands on top of the glass case and looked at Will without interest.

"I live in a dangerous neighborhood and feel the need to protect myself, I'm sorry to say," Will said.

The man reached in the display case and took out a small revolver, laying it on the case in front of Will, folding his hands again.

"A friend of mine, a fellow priest, was killed this weekend just on the street." Will picked up the gun and put his finger through the trigger hole, turning his hand so it lay in the palm. "I doubt you have many priests come in."

"They come in," the man said, almost defensively, as if his merchandise was under attack, not good enough for priests.

"I suppose the danger of cities has made that necessary," Will said.

The man took another revolver out of the case,

a larger one, opened the cylinder for Will to see how to load it, release the trigger. "I sell more of these," he said.

"I think I prefer the smaller one," Will said.

"Suit yourself." The man shrugged. "They have to be shot at close range." He put the larger revolver back in the case. "Do you know what you're doing?"

Will smiled. "I used to shoot as a boy," he said.

"I never shoot," the man said. He looked up at Will without smiling. "I've been robbed. Everyone who's got a gun shop in this town has been robbed lately," he began expanding. "Two old ladies in Arlington were shot this fall and the gunman got off with thirty handguns. Did you read that in the paper?"

In an ashtray on top of the glass case he had an apple from which he took a bite. "I don't know why two old ladies would own a gun shop. They didn't explain that in the paper."

"Maybe they were widows and the shop belonged to their husbands," Will said.

The man nodded. "Maybe," he said.

"I'd like to see how you load this gun with cartridges," Will said.

The man took the cartridges out of a drawer. "These are the ones you should use."

He looked hard at Will. "Were you in a fight?" he asked.

"A fight?"

"You have a scar on your cheek."

"Oh yes. I keep forgetting about it," Will said off-handedly. "I was in a car accident a couple of weeks ago."

"You have a lot of trouble for a priest," the man said smiling as if the thought amused him.

"Priests have trouble like everybody else, you know," Will said.

"When you come to buy the gun here, you pay in cash," the man said, ignoring the comment about priests. "I've had trouble with checks. Ever since the drug problem got bad, I can't trust a check."

"What do I need to do?" Will asked. "Just pay you, isn't that correct?"

"No, that's not correct. We've got laws." He shook his small gray head. "Priests live in towers, don't they? You don't just go out and buy a gun, cash or not," he said. "I need proof of residency in Maryland, a driver's license, although I suppose not many priests have a driver's license so a telephone or electric bill will do."

"I don't have a telephone or electric bill. The church pays for that."

"Ha," the man said. "I should have known. Living off the fat of the land."

"Not much fat on the land where I live," Will said.

That seemed to amuse the man. He made an agreeable sound in his throat. "So you live at one of those monasteries."

"Something like that. I have identification, unless I left it at home," he said, checking his pocket.

Will hesitated, his mind spinning with plans. He was uncertain what he was going to do. He had not realized that he couldn't just walk in a shop and pay with his crisp twenty-dollar bills.

"You have head priests?" the man asked, enjoying this transaction, beginning to relax.

"We do. The head priest in my monastery is called Father Seymour," Will said.

"Father Seymour," the man said. "I have a cousin named Seymour."

A plan was beginning to form in Will's head.

"What ID do you have?" the man asked. "A license?"

"A passport," Will replied.

"Are you an American citizen?"

"Of course," Will said. "I was born here in Silver Spring."

"You sound like you've got some kind of funny accent."

"That's the Silver Spring accent."

"Yeah, well, I guess I haven't heard that Silver Spring accent before." He turned to go to the back. "My wife's from Silver Spring," he said, "and her accent is southern."

What Will planned was to tell the man that after all he'd forgotten his identification and would be back later.

But the moment took on its own life. The telephone on the wall rang. When the man reached back to answer it, Will grabbed the .38 revolver and left the shop, not running initially since certainly a priest running from a gun shop would be noticed, but hurrying past the wig shop, turning right into the alley just beyond, and there he did run between the buildings, turning left where the alley turned. He heard the man shouting, or someone shouting, there was such a lot of noise on the street, and then by great good luck a taxi was letting out passengers at a light when he emerged from the alley, out of breath. He climbed in, settled deep into the back of the taxi, the revolver in his pocket.

"I wonder if you could tell me what the largest Catholic Church in town is called," Will asked, a little out of breath.

"The Shrine of the Immaculate Conception," the driver said.

"Then take me there," Will said.

"Stupid," he thought, the weight of the revolver too heavy in his trouser pocket. He had a stolen gun; he had revealed himself unnecessarily and could be in tomorrow's paper as a small item on the third page, bottom, of the Metro section. *Priest arraigned for stealing .38 revolver from local gun shop.* Or *Unidentified priest . . .* Or, worse yet, if the police were really on top of things: *William Huston of Dublin, actor, playwright, failed playwright, disguised as a Roman Catholic priest, stole a .38 revolver from a gun shop on*

Georgia Avenue in Silver Spring. Huston was caught at 3:30 in the afternoon, kneeling in the second pew of the main chapel of the Shrine of the Immaculate Conception beside the statue of the Virgin.

There was a statue of the Virgin at the Shrine. She was quite a tall woman, painted in blues and earth reds, the body of the Blessed Mother restrained, draped in deep vertical folds of wood, the face otherworldly; Will went up the side aisle and knelt in the shadow of her uninterrupted gaze.

"Forgive me, Father, for I have sinned," he began, not for any particular reason since the sanctuary he sought at the Shrine was one of personal safety, not spiritual. But he went on. "I have disguised myself as a priest, taking your name in vain" . . . on and on he went, explaining, with some relief, his situation, his forehead leaning on the knuckles of his left hand.

The church was almost empty: an elderly woman at the end of the pew in an orange paisley scarf, a sister in traditional dress crossing herself as he looked down the pew, and another priest just ahead of him standing to leave. From somewhere behind the altar he heard the monotonous Latinate chant of a priest, a sound familiar from his childhood, just the music of it, with the lilt of Irish inflection.

And suddenly the words of the confession flooded back to him without the shame he had had as a boy when the whispered "I have sinned" carried the weight of shame. Now the language seemed familial and the weight it carried for him was one of comfort, a kind of approval.

He took his hand out of his pocket, folded his arms on the pew, and rested his head in his arms.

"Forgive me, Father, for I have sinned," he said into the heat of his own breath.

Will left into the sudden sunlight of late afternoon. He turned left on Michigan Avenue, past Catholic University where he walked through the campus, pleased with his anonymity among many priests. He was glad for the sun and the sharp chill, a draft arriving with evening. He passed two priests walking together familiarly without conversation. They nodded and he nodded back. Old friends, the three of them, he pretended. He spoke to a group of women students in long pants and sweatshirts with CATHOLIC UNIVERSITY written in blue. "Good afternoon, Father," they said. A young man stopped him and asked if he knew the way to the drama department. As it happened he had passed the drama department, so he could direct the young man as if he actually belonged in this company. He could stay for weeks like this, he thought. "Professor of philosophy" perhaps, visiting from Dublin, he could say. Who was to know? Priests were by nature uninterested in matters of fact and the students would be pleased for a casual conversation with a visiting professor of philosophy. He felt entirely safe from the small man in the gun shop and somehow triumphant.

Something had changed since his arrival in Washington. Walking through the campus of Catholic University, in the cafeteria, the bookstore where he bought the Penguin edition of *Hamlet,* for a course he would be teaching at Trinity in the spring, he had a splendid feeling of confidence as if he were suddenly the one in charge of his own life on earth.

An earnest Irish girl gave him directions to the Brookland subway station—the Red Line to Shady Grove. And by the time he boarded, it was four-fifteen—one hour to the end of daylight and just over twenty-four hours until he was to meet with Michael Maguire at the Maguires' home in Georgetown.

When Will walked into the parlor of Lacey House, Father John was reading a magazine and jumped up enthusiastically.

"Aha, Father Grady," he said walking across the shadowed parlor, "exactly who I was expecting to see coming through the door. I was hoping you could have dinner with me tonight."

"That's very kind," Will said. "I wish I could."

Although he certainly knew he did not want to spend the evening with Father John, he did want to do something to keep from jumping out of his skin. "I have tickets for the opera tonight," he said without a second to invent an excuse. "Maybe tomorrow."

"Tomorrow would be very good," Father John said with a small wave of his hand. "I look forward to that."

Will nodded. Tomorrow at dinnertime, Father James Grady would be in civilian clothes on the train en route to New York City.

13

Annie showered quickly, changed to jeans and a turtleneck, watching a windstorm blow up, taking down the last of autumn. It was two-thirty. At three o'clock the children would be out of school, and at five she had to be at a rehearsal, which meant that now she had Adam's dinner to prepare—leftover chicken from Sunday—and she had to be ready for what her mother used to call "the eventualities." She sat down on the edge of the toilet and dried her hair. She'd meet the children at the corner of Fessenden and Connecticut, pick up salad and soup at the Safeway, call Continental Airlines from the phone outside the market, and arrange for two tickets to Dallas in the morning—that is, if her Visa card was not over the limit.

"I'll be right down," she called to Adam opening the door to the bathroom. She looked in the top drawer of her dresser in the bedroom where she kept her birth certificate and the children's birth certificates, her diploma from Northwestern, her Playbills through the years, and her passport from the only trip to Europe she had taken one summer when the Blakemores, in a flush of pleasure over their new grandchildren, rented a house in Tuscany and took everyone for the month of July. She dropped the birth certificates and passports into the zipper section of her bag, totaled her checkbook which showed $526.70, more than she usually had at this time of month.

"Delirious, darling," Adam called in a singsong voice from downstairs. "I seem to be having a brain hemorrhage."

"I'll be down in just a minute," Annie said ignoring the familiar comment about his terminal conditions.

"Don't get dressed," he called. "Come down naked. Hurry." His voice was sardonic. "I want to consume you."

Adam liked to talk about lovemaking but it had been a very long time since they had made love, more than a year, and mostly Annie was grateful for that—locking her desires like fortunes in her dreams. But lately Adam would awaken from a troubled sleep, grab her urgently by the shoulders, and force his erection between her small breasts until he came.

"You don't need to think of me as paraplegic, my

angel," he called again from downstairs. "Pretend I am your priest."

Annie stopped at the head of the stairs.

"Your happy birthday priest," he called. "Remember him?"

Annie sat down at the landing and put her head in her hands.

Annie had not told Adam her secrets since the accident, but when they first met, when their romance had the high excitement and danger of an unlikely union between a young baron prince and the daughter of a migrant worker from the outlaw state, she had revealed as many real secrets as she had, telling him everything, especially about the priests, like the "happy birthday priest," as she called him.

Annie was sixteen exactly and lightheaded from the pink champagne with which she and her friends at Brammel High had been celebrating her birthday during fourth period behind the science wing—when the trashcan in which she was rolling down the hill toward Primrose Street ran into Father Ian Muldoon and sent him flying. By the time she had crawled out of the trashcan, too dizzy from the ride and the champagne to stand up easily, her friends watching from the top of the hill had bolted and Annie was left to scramble unsteadily to her feet. Hours later, when she woke up, she was lying on a pull-out couch in the living room of a small dark house and Father Muldoon was packing books across from her.

Annie got up from the couch, went into the small

lavatory next to the kitchen, washed her face, brushed her hair with her fingers, straightened the tiny gossamer miniskirt she had gotten from Sylvie for her birthday, and thanked Father Muldoon for taking care of her so kindly at the moment of her terrible transgression.

"Not a transgression, my child," he said touching her hair. "A drunken spree."

"I am so sorry, Father," she said.

"Not to worry," he said. "Otherwise how would we have met?"

"I don't know," she said awkwardly. "We wouldn't have met, I suppose."

"I will be here for a few days packing up my mother's house since her death," Father Muldoon had said, "if you'd like to stop over and talk."

That was all he said, in a breezy way, a small fleshy man with a sweetness about him, a hesitation in his speech. But Annie had heard a personal exchange from him. As she walked back to the high school to collect her books, she wondered what might have happened with Father Muldoon, what he could have done to her as she lay on his couch in a champagne sleep.

"I don't understand you, Dolores Ann," Sylvie said to Annie once. "Why do you have any interest in priests?"

Annie slid down under the covers beside Sylvie so Athalia couldn't hear.

"Didn't you ever want to be an angel, Sylvie?" Annie asked. "With those sweet little wings?"

"I never did," Sylvie said. "I have never once thought about angels, even at Christmas."

"Well," Annie said burying her face in Sylvie's bony shoulder. "The reason I like priests is about angels," she whispered, "because everybody thinks I'm bad as Papa."

"No, Dolores Ann." Sylvie giggled. "Everyone *knows* you're bad as Papa."

Annie turned over on her back then, her throat full of tears like phlegm, and lay awake next to Sylvie who did not for a moment imagine the hurt her remark about badness had caused her sister.

Annie had been five, maybe younger, although she thought it must have been five because they were living in Little Rock and Ace was in the hospital from walking into a bus —and he had been drunk when the accident occurred, so Rebecca refused to visit him or to allow the children to visit him. Tom Boy, the oldest Grainey boy, now a Baptist minister in Waco, Texas, had shown signs early on of wild behavior, like Sylvie, which could have landed him as it did Sylvie in jail. But he had his siblings to satisfy his desire for trouble, putting them up to the bad behavior he would like to have done and allowing himself a clear shot at the Baptist ministry. He had Richie cutting classes in fifth grade and Sylvie drinking down the remains of the whiskey Ace kept in a bottle in his shoe, going off to second grade a little drunk. And while Ace was in the hospital, Tom Boy took Annie on the bus to St. John's Hospital downtown, gave her a note that said she was Dolores Ann Grainey and had come to visit her Papa who'd been hit by a bus, while Tom Boy sat down on the plastic seats in the reception room to wait for her. Annie remembered none of the events, although Tom Boy told her that a nurse carried her into Ace's room so she could give her father a kiss. But she did remember what happened when she came home full of excitement about her great adventure and told Rebecca.

"You heard me tell the children not to visit Papa," Rebecca said crossly. "How did you get to the hospital?"

"By bus," Annie said.

"You went on that downtown bus by yourself?"

Annie nodded, not wishing to betray Tom Boy.

"To visit Papa when I told you not to because he drank too much to see the red light when he went to cross Arrow Street and walked into a bus and fractured his skull?"

She grabbed Annie around the waist then, flung her under her arm, and carried her to the bathroom.

"You are going to take a bath," Rebecca said.

"I took a bath with Clemmie," Annie said.

"Well, that bath didn't get rid of the bad Dolores Ann, so your mama's going to give you a good bath to turn you clean."

"Clemmie did it yesterday," Annie protested.

"Clemmie didn't do it right, so it looks like I'm the only one who can do it."

What Annie remembered clear as day was standing in the bathtub while Rebecca bent over her, smelling of sweat, and scoured her arms and legs with Brillo until her skin wept.

Then her mother dried her and powdered her and dressed her. "Keep yourself clean and covered, Dolores Ann, from this day forward, until you die."

"Yes, Mama," Annie said, sitting on the edge of her bed, sunk like a small boat, the sails folded, underwater.

Even now, standing on the bus downtown, in the kitchen making supper, walking with Lexa and Nich-o on a beautiful day, she would feel a wave of desolation, out of nowhere, swing over her and she'd have to stop and sit down, as if her heart were giving out.

Somewhere at the center Annie Blakemore believed she was bad beyond forgiveness.

Later on the evening of Rebecca's bathing, Annie had come to the dinner table in disguise. Sylvie told the story often, how funny it was. And Athalia told it too—how shameful.

Even in the days when there was hardly food to eat at the Graineys', Rebecca insisted that they all sit at dinner together—except Ace who was commonly drunk by dinner and did not eat—and they'd sit around the long Formica table in the kitchen with bowls of white bean soup and bread, and while the soup cooled Rebecca would say a long prayer about the food which was never good enough to be thankful for, so Tom Boy said. This particular dinner, Annie sat quietly at the table, her hands folded on the edge, a sheet over her head.

"I'll have you take that sheet off your head before we thank the good Lord for our supper, Dolores Ann," Rebecca said.

"It's not a sheet," Annie said. "I am a ghost and that is why I look this way."

"Real ghosts are dead people," Athalia said. "And you are Dolores Ann Grainey as usual."

"No," Annie said. "The dear Lord, who knows everything and sees everything, our good behavior and our bad behavior, like Mama says, knows I am a ghost."

Adam was in the kitchen smoking a cigarette when Annie went downstairs.

He grabbed her waist as she walked by him and pushed his arm into her pubic bone.

"I want you to tell me who you've fallen in love with," he said to her, straightforward without the familiar lilt of sarcasm in his tone.

"Don't be silly," Annie said.

"I am not being silly, Annie," he said quietly. "You have fallen in love with someone."

He pulled her down on his lap. "Kiss me," he said, his arm tight around her waist, pressing hard against her rib cage.

"Please Adam."

"Please what?" he said. "Please kiss me?"

"No," she said.

He held her tighter. "Please don't kiss me. Right? Please forgive me is what you meant to say, isn't that right, Delirious?"

"Adam, you're hurting me."

He took hold of her face and kissed her hard until, with a kind of desperation, she relaxed against his chest.

"So," he said running his long fingers through his hair. "Tell me what is going on with you."

Annie straightened her skirt, folded her hands in her lap as if she were in church. "I was thinking of giving you leftover chicken for dinner unless you'd like me to pick something up at the Safeway," she said evenly.

He pushed her off his lap and looked at her with an unfamiliar expression although he was smiling.

"Leftover chicken sounds perfectly marvelous, Annie," he said. "I'll eat it and think of you." He wheeled his chair into the living room and turned on the radio full volume.

14

Will lay on the bed at number 11 Lacey House in the early dark of five o'clock. The light in his room was off to discourage a visitation by Father John and he lay in his undershorts and a tee shirt, one arm under his head as a pillow, the hand of the other on the revolver beside him under the sheet.

He had played the role of a killer only twice in his career, most recently as Macey Barone in *The Death of the First Wife* by a young Irish playwright, and that role had been a difficult one to play. Macey's capacity for violence was so subtly portrayed, so unlikely, there was a tendency for the killing itself, when it occurred at the end of the first act, to seem melodramatic and cost the players the audience's belief in the story.

A calm settled over Will. He found himself thinking, actually thinking for the first time since his arrival in the United States, thinking now about his work and the fact of being an actor. What counted in theater, perhaps in everything what counted, was authority. In theater it was the authority of the writer first, and then the actor and finally the audience, its willingness to allow the illusion of the play to carry the day.

There had been few unguarded moments in Will's life when he had not been dressed for the occasion.

He had never had a real love affair, never allowed himself the range of feelings, the risk of raw exposure of the heart. Although he had felt strongly in the last twenty years, his feelings were arranged by whatever role he had to play. The only authentic moment of his adult life that he could remember, that he could believe in, had been the death of Jamey.

If this moment were a play and not Will Huston's life at all, then his role would be to avenge his brother's death. Although he could not recover Jamey's lost life, he could set the world of his small territory in order once again.

And if he killed Michael Maguire on Thursday, the twenty-first of November 1991, between six and seven in the evening, what chance then of his actual survival as a free man? Could he kill him quickly, run out the back door of the

Maguires' house on Reservoir Road, run down the street to Wisconsin Avenue, get a taxi to Union Station, get his belongings in locker A270, change, dump his priest's costume in the trashbasket, get on the train to New York City, spend the night at Brendan's and the next full day as an ordinary man in New York City, get on the six o'clock for Dublin, go back to the flat on Archduke as an unencumbered civilian, Will Huston, actor, playwright, et cetera?

Will considered the dangers of his plan. Tomorrow during the day, he would have to check the back of the house on Reservoir Road and determine how best to escape.

He heard footsteps up the stairs, along the corridor, and there was a knock at his door.

"Father Grady." It was the voice of Father John.

At first Will didn't reply, although he was going to have to say something since Father John had seen him come upstairs.

"Excuse me, Father Grady," Father John said. "Are you there?"

Will put his pillow over his face. "Yes," he said, his voice muffled in foam rubber. He made the sound of waking from a deep sleep.

"Oh, I'm terribly sorry," Father John said. "I just wanted a word with you before you left for the opera."

"In a bit, Father," Will said.

"Of course," Father John said. "Just knock on my door before you leave."

Will waited for the footsteps down the hall, the door of Father John's room to open and close. Then he turned on his light, got up, made the bed, and pulled on his trousers. He put the gun in his pocket, and over his civilian clothes he buttoned his cassock.

The door to Father John's room was open when Will went down the hall to the bathroom. He could see him reading in a chair and waved. In the bathroom, he splashed water on his face avoiding the scar, ran his fingers through the hair of his gray wig.

"Come in, Father," Father John said to him as he went back down the corridor. "Sit down."

Will sat in the high-back chair of the desk, noticing as he sat the brightness of the reading light turned at an angle toward him, so he turned it away.

"I have never developed a taste for the opera," Father John said. He was reading a detective novel and put it on the desk, crossing his legs, folding his hands in his lap.

"I love high excitement experienced by others." Will smiled. "That is what I like in opera."

"I'm afraid I'm very pedestrian and like movies better. I find I go to sleep at plays."

"It's easy to go to sleep at plays," Will said. "Theaters are kept so hot."

"I'm sorry to have wakened you," Father John said. "But I wanted to thank you today and to tell you as well what has transpired since I saw you."

"Of course."

"I saw the young girl today at lunch."

"Yes."

"We met at a restaurant on R Street in Georgetown and she told me she was having difficulty with her studies because of me." He seemed entirely pleased with this confidence although he assumed a demeanor of great seriousness.

"You've met often?" Will asked.

"She was in my parish in Minneapolis."

"So she's falling in love with you."

"She says she is, I am chagrined to tell you. I said nothing myself. She thinks I am here for a conference." He took a deep breath. "She tells me," he said and rushed on, "she's a virgin and I find myself thinking—with a virgin."

"That it would be different, more acceptable with a virgin."

He hesitated. "Isn't it awful, but that's exactly how I've been thinking." He blew his nose. "Really, Father— things in my mind are quite out of hand. I find myself thinking how much more attractive she is to me knowing that she is a virgin."

"Of course," Will said. "I know exactly what you mean. I am reminded of a story of a man who could only love virgins and there were no virgins in the world." It was quite a lengthy story, taking all the time before he had to leave for the opera, but he continued in spite of Father John's growing boredom. And then at six he got up to leave.

"I am off to dinner now and then the opera," Will said. "And I'll see you for dinner tomorrow night. It will have to be late as I'm meeting someone for a drink around six."

"Then we'll have dinner at eight," Father John said standing to walk with Will to the door.

Standing room was sold out for *Don Giovanni*.

"I'm so sorry, Father," the woman at the ticket window said. "You could just go to the usher and see if someone doesn't show."

It was seven forty-five, too early to go back to Lacey House, and he didn't want to walk around alone in Washington. The weather had turned cold and damp, the atmosphere was gloomy, and he had a sense of doom. Better the company of strangers at the Kennedy Center with all its theaters lit than walking alone through an unfamiliar city with a gun in his pocket. He walked down the flat maroon carpet toward the Opera House, milling amongst the crowd gathered under the glittering lights, drinking wine in clear plastic goblets, chattering quietly. He was the only priest that he could see and he felt suddenly conspicuous in his cassock so he made himself busy, buying a program and some cigarettes, a box of chocolate-covered peanuts. He stood on the steps to the theater as people filed by him with their tickets. Across the hall he saw a young boy, but too far away for him to tell his age, standing in a group of adults, his legs apart, his toes pointed in, looking up at the grown-ups, and with a rush of warmth Will was reminded of the boy the night before.

It would be pleasant to see that child again, he thought, to pass the time with him. He found himself eased just by the thought of it, wondering if his decision to come to the opera for the second night was actually a wish to see the boy. He finished his chocolate peanuts and threw the box in the trash, lit a cigarette. The foyer was emptying. It was almost eight o'clock. At eight, he went to the usher at the center door and said that standing room had been sold out but on the chance someone did not show up, the pleasant woman at the ticket office had suggested he check with the usher. The usher, a woman, middle-aged, dark, dumpy with bright pink cheeks, possibly Irish, smiled warmly at him.

"Of course, Father," she said. "I will do what I can. You just wait until everyone is in and then we'll see if we can squeeze you in the back." She touched his arm. "No need to pay."

He lit another cigarette and lost himself in the crowd as they went into the theater. There was a tall, preternaturally tall woman, not young, her hair dyed too black. She was dressed in a lavender silk dress and high heels, a kind of tropical bird looming over the small plump man whose arm was looped through hers. And a young, anxious woman awkward with her escort, following behind a strange and beautiful woman who had shaved her head and wore a rhinestone tiara. The foyer almost bare, Will went back up the steps where the usher with whom he had spoken stood quite solitary now in her red jacket, her arm full of programs.

"Now, Father," she took him by the elbow and guided him through the main doors, holding the interior door open for him. The orchestra was playing when he went in and the hall was dark.

"Just slip in," she whispered.

He moved to the back, leaning against the wall. Although tall, he was not tall enough to see over the group in front of him so he steadied himself against the wall in case he should fall dead asleep with nervous exhaustion. He closed his eyes.

At first he did not feel anything. Then it seemed as if the woman just in front of him was stepping on him and he moved his foot back. He heard "Father." And when he looked down, it was at the boy he had met the night before.

His heart leapt for joy.

The boy scrambled to his feet and leaned against the wall next to Will.

"Remember me?" he whispered.

"Of course." Will nodded, leaning down so they could hear each other above the sound of the music.

"I thought you might be here because you said last night that some priests like operas."

"And I thought you might be here because you are an opera connoisseur."

"That's right, I am," the boy said.

"And is your mother singing tonight?"

"No, she's not," he said. "Last night was her big chance. It almost never happens."

"Well, I'm very glad to see you," Will said resting his hand on the boy's shoulder lightly, not to insinuate himself. He gave the gesture consideration—he wanted the boy to know that they had the beginning of a friendship.

"My sister's here," the boy said pointing toward the railing. *"Don Giovanni* is her favorite. Mine is *Aida."*

"You told me."

"With the elephants."

"You said that too."

"I never change my mind," the boy said.

They stood together without talking the whole of the first act, the boy leaning against his side. Will couldn't concentrate on the music; he was thinking what he could say to this child during intermission. Such a very long time since he'd been around children. Last night, there had been a purpose to their conversation because he was taking the boy to the men's room and they had just met, but now they would have twenty minutes of conversation and they knew each other, not as strangers exactly, but only enough to be awkward with one another, and if they were awkward, Will thought, what a loss of this chance to have a brief friendship slipped into the middle of a life. The idea appealed to Will.

He could ask questions. People love to answer questions, especially about themselves, but would a child want to answer questions about himself? Would that be an invasion? Perhaps he would prefer to hear stories. Slightly outrageous stories struck Will as the right sort for a boy his age and he tried to remember stories from his own childhood—stories his mother or Bernadette had told him, stories from grammar school, stories he used to tell to Jamey when they lay in the dark in the cold damp room they shared above the kitchen of Mailbones Pub. The memory of winter dampness, of that small room smelling of pork rolls and meat pies, brought with it the sudden sweetness of Jamey in the cot next to his bed.

Just as the lights went up in the Opera House, he remembered a moment sitting with Jamey early in the morning on one of the bar stools in the pub—where they often ate when the pub was closed. It was winter, bitter cold and damp. Jamey was wrapped in a blanket and they sat side by side drinking coffee, their hands around the mugs to warm them.

"Tell me a story about porcupines," Jamey had asked.

"I don't know any stories about porcupines," Will said.

"Make one up," he said.

Will blew his hot breath into the coffee. "There was a porcupine," he began, "who was a butcher in the village where he lived and well thought of by most of the people in the village although not well understood, which is the case with porcupines.''

"He shouldn't be a butcher," Jamey said. "It is foolish to think of the porcupine as a butcher."

"This is my story, Jamey, and in my story he is a butcher."

"But you are telling the story for me," Jamey said, "and I want him to be the postman so people will like him better even though they don't understand him."

"In the village of Drew in Northern Ireland," Will began again, "there lived seventeen people and fourteen animals and amongst the animals was Padraic Porcupine, who was an agreeable, well-liked, misunderstood porcupine who had the position of postman for Drew."

James settled comfortably against Will.

"Life for Padraic was uneventful except for the occasional love letter that Bernadette O'Malley received from her suitor in the town of Killarney and which Padraic, as postman, opened and read aloud to himself and then resealed and delivered to Bernadette. 'My darling Bernadette, light of my eyes, flower of my soul, cushion of my ailing heart. I count the hours until we meet again and kiss beneath the lamp so I can gaze into your lavender eyes.' ''

"Not a gooey story," Jamey said.

"That's almost the end of the gooey part," Will said. " 'I hope we will be married by spring in the garden of your mother's house full of the scent of lilacs. Forever, my beloved, Paul.' ''

Will would have gone on with the story then if his mother had not come downstairs from the Hustons' living quarters above the pub and told Jamey to hustle up or he'd be late for school and asked Will to lay the fire. Several times in the next week, Jamey asked Will to tell him the rest of the story or asked him what happened to Padraic or whether anyone ever found out that he was reading the love letters of Bernadette O'Malley, but soon Will went back to university for the spring term and after that the subject of porcupines did not come up again.

"My mother gave me five dollars for treats," the boy said when the first act was over. "Would you like a treat?"

His sister had moved over to where the boy was standing with Will and said in a quiet voice, but Will could hear her, that he should not have anything to drink during intermission because he would have to use the bathroom in the middle of the second act.

"I can hold it a long time, Lexa," the boy said. "Or else if I can't, Father will take me to the men's room."

The girl smiled up at Will.

"I saw you last night," she said.

"And I saw you last night. What a coincidence," Will said. "Would you like to come with us to get a drink?"

"No," the girl said. "Thank you." She looked up at him. "Do you remember my name?"

"No. We didn't exchange names last night. My name is Father James."

"His name is Nicholas and my name is Alexandra," the girl said.

"Those are very grand names," Will said.

"That's because my mother likes to be Russian," Nicholas said.

"And our father says our mother is really one hundred percent Texan," Alexandra said.

"She likes to be Russian better," Nicholas said. "Have you ever been to Texas?"

"Never," Will said.

"We have to take our vacations there with Aunt Clementine," Nicholas said. "It's not so much fun."

They waited in a very long line for drinks, the boy standing quietly next to Will, leaning occasionally against him. Once he actually buried his face into the cassock and Will kept very still, even allowing the line to advance without him, not to ruin the sweetness of the moment.

"Tomorrow I won't see you if you come to the opera," Nicholas said after they had gotten cider.

"I'm very sorry to hear that," Will said.

"Tomorrow we have to go to Texas to visit my Aunt Clementine for the weekend," he said. "And maybe we'll go see Aunt Sylvie in jail," he added.

"Poor Aunt Sylvie," Will said. "Has she been in jail for a long time?"

"Sometimes she's in jail and sometimes she's not," Nicholas said. "But I like her best of all the aunts and uncles even though she's a druggie, Mama says." They leaned against the wall of the lobby drinking hot apple cider, sharing a box of chocolate-covered peanuts. "My father never comes to Texas."

"He doesn't like Texas?" Will asked.

"He had his accident in Texas and now he's in a wheelchair." The boy was pensive. "Do you have children?"

"I don't," Will said. "Priests don't, you know."

"I didn't know that," Nicholas said. "We don't go to church." He reached up and took Will's hand, not to hold it exactly although that may have been what he had initially in mind, but he turned it over in his own hand, ran his fingers along the elevated blue veins, pressed his thumb into the center of Will's palm as if he were accustomed to a particular reaction in the soft flesh. "Do you like *Don Giovanni*?" he asked.

"Very much," Will said.

"The soprano's voice hurt my ears." Nicholas dropped Will's hand. "Maybe I'll sit out in the lobby during the next act. Besides, it's too hot in there."

"It is hot," Will said.

"Maybe you'd like to sit out here with me," Nicholas said, "and I'll tell you about my father's accident."

"That would be very interesting," Will said. "I'd like to hear about your father's accident."

But as it turned out, the subject of Nicholas's father did not come up although they didn't return to the performance of *Don Giovanni*. Instead they sat on the maroon

136.

carpeted floor of the large empty foyer and Will told the story of Padraic Porcupine straight to the end.

"So," Will said inventing the rest of the story from where he left off with Jamey, "Padraic was very pleased to have read the love letters of Bernadette O'Malley, but not wishing to be discovered as untrustworthy in his job he began to have dreams of his very own Bernadette to whom he could write such lovely letters."

"So he meets her after work at the TCBY yogurt shop," Nicholas said. "She is having chocolate swirl with granola jimmies and he orders the same thing."

"Exactly," Will said putting his arm on Nicholas's knee. "And they sit down across from each other at a little white table and he says 'I am Padraic Porcupine' and she says 'I am Lucinda Porcupine' and they kiss."

"Good," Nicholas said. "And she turns into a beautiful princess with yellow curls and he turns into a hero." He yawned, leaning against Will's arm. "What time is it?"

"Ten-thirty," Will said.

"Is there time for another story?"

"We should go in and see the end," Will said standing up, and as he did he saw a man in a wheelchair, quite a nice-looking man, youngish, or a little younger than Will, with red hair and a squarish, speckled beard. But something in the swiftness of his approach, right toward where Will was standing with Nicholas, or the look of strangeness on the man's face as he got closer, was alarming.

Nicholas grabbed Will's cassock. "That's my father,"

he said, the color drained from his face. "He never leaves the house." He looked up at Will. "He never never leaves the house."

"Nicholas," the man said, and he was upon them before Will had a chance to leave.

"What are you doing out here during the performance?" the man asked.

"I was talking to the priest," Nicholas said quietly.

"Hello," Will said. "I'm Father James Grady and we were both a bit too hot in the theater."

The man looked at Will with an expression of confusion, even, Will thought later, derangement—it was hard to tell.

"You are a Catholic priest," the man said.

"I am," Will said.

"Do you know my wife?"

"No," Will said, perplexed by such a question. "I don't know your wife. I don't even know your son," he added, sensing that his association with Nicholas might cause trouble for the boy. "We just met at the opera and struck up a conversation."

"Well, it's very peculiar," the man said, "and I don't actually believe you."

"It's true," Will said. "Absolutely true."

But he did not wish to linger with this man and excused himself for the men's room.

"Could he take me to the men's, Papa?" Nicholas

asked as Will left. "It would be easier for him than for you and I have to go."

"No," Nicholas's father said. "He is a stranger."

"Good-bye, Nicholas," Will said. "It was a pleasure to meet you." Will went into the men's room on the orchestra level, into one of the cubicles, and sat down. Probably the father would bring Nicholas to the men's room and he did not wish to be seen by either of them— the boy with his sudden attachment to Will or the crippled man with his unaccountable anger.

Will rearranged his wig. No one had come in and by his watch he had been waiting for almost ten minutes. He washed his hands under the warm water thoroughly as if they were soiled, dried them under the blower, patted the revolver in his pocket, and left.

When he came out of the men's room into the large foyer of the Opera House, no one was there except an elderly usher sitting on a fold-out chair by the telephone with his eyes closed. Will hurried down the hall past the ticket office and out the main door where a line of taxis was waiting for the end of the opera.

15

Annie lay on the floor of the Opera House dressing room, her eyes closed, her feet against the wall. Marcia, in a long satin dress and crinolines, playing tonight the role of Donna Elvira, knelt beside her.

"It feels like a heart attack," Annie said thinly. Certainly her chest felt stretched tight across the sternum, her breath shallow, almost no breath at all.

"You're not having a heart attack," Beatrice, in her role as the peasant girl Zerlina, herself bent over with cramps, said to Annie. "You're premenopausal."

"I think we should call an ambulance," Marcia said.

"You always think there's a state of emergency," Beatrice said. "This is hyperventilation. You know that, Annie." She checked the lipsticks on the dressing table and without looking in the mirror spread bright red across her lips. "Hyperventilation from too much carbon dioxide going out and too much oxygen in the brain. This must have happened to you millions of times. You're a singer."

"I'm glad you're not my mother, Beatrice," Marcia said. "Do you think this is an emergency?" she asked Annie quietly. "Or do you want to try to breathe into a paper bag in case you have hyperventilated?"

"I don't know," Annie said, tears gathering behind her eyelids, her heart dancing above her rib cage as if it would fly out of her chest. Certainly it was something taking over the machinery of her body, she thought. Either too much oxygen or a heart attack or Adam or the priest. She sat up on her elbow. In the distance, as if the sound were traveling underwater, she thought she heard her name. "Annie Blakemore, please." And someone was knocking on the dressing room door.

"Annie Blakemore," Beatrice said in a singsong voice. "Annie Blakemore is here," and she opened the door.

"Annie Blakemore, guess what?" she said. "Your husband in the flesh."

"Annie doesn't feel very well," Marcia said to Adam, but Annie was on her feet.

"I'm okay," she said. "I'm really okay," and she slipped into the corridor where Adam sat in his wheelchair, his hair wild, the collar of his trench coat up, and beside him Nicholas, white-faced, standing very still and straight.

"Papa called a taxi and the taxi driver carried him down the steps and drove him here by surprise," Nicholas said quietly.

"I didn't know you had any plans to come," Annie said.

"Of course I had no plans to come, darling." Adam pulled Nicholas onto his lap. "And then Continental Airlines called to say that the flight for Nicholas and Alexandra had been changed and would be departing from National Airport tomorrow morning at eight forty-five instead of eight fifty-seven as previously scheduled."

Annie leaned against the wall.

"Imagine my surprise," Adam said. "I wanted to get that news to you as soon as possible."

"They are going to see Clementine for the weekend," Annie said defensively.

"It must have slipped your mind, Delirious," Adam said. "You never mentioned it to me."

"I thought I had, Adam," Annie said. "So much has happened this week."

"Places," Marcia called, opening the door of the dressing room. "Curtain, everyone."

"I'll be waiting after the show with Nich-o and Lexa," Adam said.

"You'll be waiting here?"

"Right here, my darling," Adam said. "By your sweet side for the rest of my life."

Annie closed the door to the dressing room and sat down in a chair by the stage door. "I can't breathe," she said.

"Of course you can breathe," Marcia said. "Deep breaths. Through your nose, into a paper bag."

"He's not what I expected," Beatrice said pensively.

"I told you he was in a wheelchair, didn't I?" Annie leaned her head against the wall.

"Yes," Beatrice said. "You did say about the wheelchair." She touched Annie's cheek. "He didn't seem on first glance to be the husband you would have."

"We should never have married," Annie said. She stood up and took a deep breath. "But we did. And that's that."

Annie and Adam had married at St. Peter's Episcopal Church in Essex at a small ceremony conducted by Adam's cousin, attended by several of Adam's friends from boarding school, his aunts and uncles, friends of his parents in Essex, and Sylvie who arrived in Essex by train during one of her drying out periods dressed in a small shimmering silver dress that dipped almost to the nipples of her pale white breasts.

"You must have a member of your family in attendance," Gail Blakemore had said. "However," as she told

Adam later at the reception and in full hearing of Annie, "I should have thought better of it, considering Annie's family."

The wedding was Adam's punishment.

"You have to marry me," he'd said after the accident. "You're responsible."

"I want to marry you," she said. "That's all I ever wanted." Which was true. From the first time she saw him onstage at Northwestern, she had wanted to marry Adam Blakemore. There was a wildness about him, the early seeds of his present madness—an irreverence, a cocky disclaimer of responsibility for ordinary behavior. At the time she found him masculine, like Ace in a way. She had not understood the personal safety of money and upbringing, which the Blakemores had, knowing no one in Texas, especially in Brammel, who had neither, just a hodgepodge of mixed Americans, like leftover suppers, trying to get on with their lives. So Adam was a new breed. Even his bemusement at her deceptive simplicity was attractive to her as if they were foreigners in a romance of uncommon language. His contempt for her unsophisticated manner was first evident at visits to his family's house in Connecticut. And then in Brammel. But their love affair had been over the afternoon at Clementine's before the accident. When Adam recovered enough to be moved from the hospital in Dallas to New York City, he said that Annie should come along. That she should stay with him until he recovered completely and was free to make his own arrangements. And if he did not recover completely, then she should stay with him indefinitely.

She agreed. It was not even a question of agreement. She felt too terrible about what had happened, was too stunned by the horror of what was not entirely an accident on the freeway outside of Dallas. She couldn't separate from Adam so they were bound together as if the skin of one had been grafted on the raw, exposed skin of the other for life.

There were days after the accident, especially when they were in New York City at Juilliard and after Nicholas was born, Adam writing plays at the desk in their bedroom, when Annie was afraid he had lost his senses. But her real fear of his dissolution, the loss of sanity which seemed to accompany him now, like scent, came in slowly like a winter fog and settled around her in disguise.

After *Don Giovanni,* they took a taxi home, the four of them locked in the backseat together, Alexandra between Adam and Annie, Nicholas on Annie's lap, the wheelchair folded, slid in front of Adam.

"A night at the theater, eh?" the cabdriver said cheerfully. "Now that's a thing I've never done. Gone to the theater with my wife and children."

"We do it often," Adam said pleasantly.

"It must cost a bundle."

"It does," Adam said. "But we save up."

"My mama's in the theater," Nicholas said. "We go for free."

"So you're a movie star?" the driver asked.

This seemed to amuse Adam and he laughed gaily, lifting Annie's hand and kissing it in a grand gesture.

"Entirely right," he said. "You've probably heard of her. Delirious Blakemore?"

"Delirious Blakemore?"

"Do you know that name?"

"I don't believe I've ever heard the name Delirious," the driver said. "It doesn't actually even sound like a name."

"Well it is," Adam said. "It's the name of my darling wife."

"It's not, Papa," Nicholas said quietly. "Her name is Annie Blakemore."

Later, in the kitchen, the children in pajamas sitting at the table with hot chocolate, Adam brought up his plans to leave.

"I am planning a trip," he said. Annie was sitting at the table, her feet on Alexandra's chair.

"A trip?" she asked.

"Tomorrow. Just like Nicholas and Alexandra. I thought I mentioned it to you."

She looked at him oddly. "Perhaps you did," she

said. She could be as strange as he could be, she decided. She could remember anything, whether it had happened or not. "But I've forgotten where you said you were going."

"Paris," he said.

Nicholas looked up from his hot chocolate. "Mama said we would go to Paris someday and have coffee in the cafés."

"Well, you're welcome to come with me, Nich-o," Adam said. "It might be better than the weekend in Dallas with Aunt Clementine."

Nicholas put his nose in the steam from the hot chocolate and lowered his eyes.

"So, Nicholas, what do you think? Just you and me in Paris for a week."

Annie felt the sudden faintness of this evening in the dressing room at the Kennedy Center and, agitated, got up, poured a glass of orange juice and drank it slowly, her back to the children.

"Thank you very much, Papa," Nicholas said quietly. "But I promised Aunt Clementine I'd come to Dallas."

"People die in Dallas," Adam said lifting his lifeless leg across the other leg. "President Kennedy did." And he wheeled his chair behind Nicholas, his arm around his son's neck in what might have seemed under normal circumstances to be a gesture of fun, but these were not normal circumstances. Nicholas slid under his father's grasp to the floor, holding his neck.

"What were you doing?" Nicholas asked his father, scrambling up beside Annie.

"I was hugging you, Nicholas," Adam said calmly. "What did you think I was trying to do?"

"Nich-o thought you were trying to strangle him," Alexandra said.

"Nicholas?" Adam said touching his son's arm. "Is that right?"

Nicholas hesitated. He took Alexandra's hand.

"No," he said in careful self-defense. "Good night, Mama." He followed his sister out of the kitchen. "Good night, Papa."

Annie put the empty hot chocolate cups in the dishwasher, wiped the table, put out cat food for Brunnhilde and Siegfried.

"I hold you responsible for this," Adam said.

Annie did not reply. She seemed to be standing in the center of a hurricane, at the actual center so the storm where she stood was a point of calm, an island of safety if she didn't move into the high winds around her.

Adam had lost his mind. That was clear. If she could last until morning, if they all could, holding to the pretense of an ordinary life, treat him as if his behavior were the behavior of a perfectly sane man, then tomorrow, when she left to take the children to the airport, they would all disappear.

"Would you like me to help you upstairs?" Annie asked.

Adam looked at her with a cockeyed smile.

"That would be adorable of you, Delirious, my Delirious," he began to sing. "My own sweet Delirious, Delirious of my heart."

The children were in bed with their lights out when she went upstairs, and she went into each room, kneeling down next to the bed.

"What is the matter with Papa?" Lexa asked. "He doesn't make sense."

"I know, darling," Annie said. "He's not very well." She took Alexandra's hand. "If we have to leave in a hurry tonight because we are worried about Papa, then I want you to be ready."

"Are you going to tell Nich-o, too?"

"No, I'm not going to worry him. I'd like you to help with Nich-o if necessary."

Annie ran her fingers quickly across Alexandra's back, kissed her hair, and stood.

"You don't have time to scratch my back?"

"Tomorrow," Annie said. "Now I should go to Papa."

"You could sleep with me," Nicholas said when Annie came in to kiss him good night.

"Maybe later," Annie said. "If I can't get to sleep."

"I'm not going to sleep tonight at all," Nicholas said. And as she left the room he asked her to leave the bathroom light on and his door open.

When she went back into their bedroom, Adam was sitting in bed reading *Riders to the Sea*. He smiled at her when she came in. "This is quite a good play, you know," he said pleasantly as if nothing whatsoever had happened that night.

"Is it?" Annie asked lightly. "I've never read it."

"We should do it together," Adam said. "When I return from Paris."

It was after one when Adam finished reading the play and turned out the light. Annie was wide awake. When she closed her eyes, the priest floated along the horizon of her mind's eye and Annie swam up behind him, put her arms around his waist.

"Hello," she whispered into his ear, blowing her breath light as petals on his neck.

"My darling," he said turning and putting his arms around her, lifting her up, kissing her softly on the lips, brushing his lips across her face, in her hair. "I have wondered where you were," he said running his tongue along the inside of her lips. "And would you ever return?"

"I am here," Annie said. She unbuttoned the front of her knit dress until it fell open, untied the silk scarf around her neck, and dropped it to the floor. The priest took off his collar, undid the cassock, pulling it over his head, ruffling his hair.

"Close your eyes," he said.

She closed her eyes. He took the dress off her shoulders, pulled down her half slip, undid her bra, pulled her panties to the floor. "Step out," he said kissing her belly with his tongue. She stepped out, standing now in just her lace-up boots. "Now open your eyes," he said.

He had taken off his cassock and stood naked, a spread of black hair graying on his chest, and a large simple cross, like a tattoo but too natural in appearance to have been burned there, went from the top of his chest to below his navel and across the width of him from arm to arm.

"You are so beautiful," he said and lifted her in the air above his head as if she had no weight, bringing her down on him slowly until he filled her.

Adam's sleep was troubled; he was speaking in what sounded like another language.

"Mama," Alexandra called.

Annie looked in her room.

"What's happening with Papa?" she asked.

"He's talking in his sleep," Annie said.

"I know that," Lexa said. "I've been listening to him."

Annie went into Lexa's room, sat down on the side of her bed, and rubbed her arm.

"Papa was saying 'Delirious,' " Lexa said. "I hate the way he calls you that."

"He says it as a joke," Annie said.

"It's not a joke."

Pale light from the window fell across Alexandra's

face, only half of it, distorting the shape, and Annie leaned over to kiss the side of her cheek in shadow.

"Do you think he is going to Paris tomorrow?"

"I don't know, Lexa," Annie said. "Sometimes I don't understand your father."

Alexandra turned over on her stomach. "Now would you scratch my back, Mama?" said asked. "I can't sleep."

Annie crossed her legs and, resting her elbows on her knees, scratched Lexa's back, absently, listening to Adam tossing in bed, not moaning exactly, but the pitch of his voice was unnaturally high and the words indistinct.

"Did Nich-o tell you we saw the same priest again at *Don Giovanni?*"

"He didn't say."

"The priest likes us," Lexa said.

"How do you know?"

"You can tell," Alexandra said. "Like you can tell that lately Papa doesn't."

"Papa loves you," Annie said, but she knew that for a long time, maybe years, Adam's connection to the real world did not include love.

"Maybe," Alexandra said. "But he doesn't like you so much anymore."

Siegfried jumped on the bed and curled up in Annie's lap, licking his belly.

"Tell me more about the priest you met," Annie said. "Ever since I was a little girl, I have been interested in priests."

"I forget," Lexa said sleepily. "He's just a nice priest." She rubbed her arm across her eyes. "And he wears a wig."

"A wig?" Annie asked. "How do you know he wears a wig?"

"I can tell. I always know when people are wearing wigs."

Adam called out in his sleep, loud and very clear. "Squash" is what he said.

"Try to go to sleep," Annie whispered to Alexandra. "I'm going in with Papa."

"Maybe soon we'll really go to Paris," Alexandra said quietly. "Do you think?"

"I hope," Annie said, wondering in the mysterious way of silent conversation whether Paris had come to mean the same for Alexandra as it did for her.

In the kitchen she brushed cat hairs off her night-gown, made hot chocolate, and then sat in the dark in the living room, too wide awake to sleep, thinking of her father. Annie was not a reflective person in an ordinary way. She did not have a tendency to fret or consider days to rearrange their conclusions. She thought of the accident with Adam but always with a sense of inevitability so that if the conditions were the same as they had been that summer afternoon in Dallas, the accident would happen again exactly as it had. She had too much energy to be a fatalist, too little interest in unhappiness. But she did imagine windows of escape, actually believing that it was only a matter of time before she and Lexa and Nich-o were seated in the center aisle, front row, of a wide-bodied jet sailing east above the Atlantic Ocean. What reflection Annie did have was hidden in the narrative of her imagination.

Upstairs, Adam was out of bed. Annie heard him get in his wheelchair and cross the floor of their bedroom to the bathroom. He didn't call. Ordinarily if he woke up to find her absent, he would call. She listened but she didn't want to go upstairs, to face his questions—what was she doing up and who was it preoccupying her imagination? She lay very quietly against the cushions of the couch, her knees under her nightgown, her hands over her mouth so she didn't hear her own breathing. The wheelchair crossed the bedroom floor again, out into the hall, to the top of the steps, and she expected to hear his call—''Delirious'' or ''Annie,'' spoken crossly. ''Can't you hear I'm up?''

The sound of the wheelchair, the swish of rubber on the hardwood floor stopped and she was just about to get up, to go to the bottom of the stairs to see what was going on, when there was a loud thump against the stairs. By the time she reached the hallway and turned on a light, the wheelchair had tumbled down the steps and Adam lay face down at the bottom of the steps, a slender stream of blood coming from his mouth.

16

Will couldn't sleep. He lay in the narrow bed, his arms
folded behind his head, his legs crossed at the ankles, waiting for morning which promised to be a long time coming.
Hadn't he read someplace just recently about raising your
arms above your heart—or was it crossing your arms? Perhaps it was an article in the Sunday supplement of the
Dublin Times on ways to avoid heart attacks. Putting your
arms above your head was not advised, he remembered,
folding his arms now across his chest.

He didn't know what to do with the revolver which
lay in the folds of his cassock assuming a presence the size
of a large beast seated across from him in the small bedroom, number 11 Lacey House. He needed to read. He

read from the Penguin edition of *Hamlet,* the op-ed page of the *Washington Post* for November 20, 1991, and looked at a copy of *Life* magazine with a familiar picture from the sixties of John Kennedy with his handsome Irish face, the shock of hair, a certain humor in his expression. He did not have the look of a man acquainted with violence.

Outside his room, the light was on, shining through the slit under his door, and Will knew that Father John was sitting in the chair in his bedroom reading with the door open—just in case Will had to pee and Father John could catch him unawares. "One small thing, Father James," Father John would say leaping to his feet, "about the girl."

He missed Maud. It was not so much that he wanted her in particular but just the familiarity of her voice in the kitchen, the heat of her body next to his, although they had not slept together for years—but he remembered what living with a woman could be, especially in winter when the weather sank to the bone.

He wished, in an abstract way, that he had wanted to marry her, that they had wanted to marry each other—not for the marriage exactly although certainly he would be lonely if Maud were not in the flat when he went back to Dublin, especially on the long days before rehearsals, sitting over a play he was writing at the kitchen table with black coffee and a cigarette, a disappearing sense of the story he was trying to write. And who would be there to listen? It was not even Maud he missed but the chance he had with her for a child.

He missed a child. That is what he wished for in his life, a long kite string to his own fortune flying from the sweet body of a child, a sense of redemption and well-being, a belief that the world as he found it was a good place to live a life.

Until he was thirteen, he had believed in God. The daily order of church, the mass and confession and communion, the changing of the seasons, the familiarity of the language gave him a sense of power. Even on the worst of days, he could, if he confessed his sins, feel asense of victory. That was not the intent of the Roman Catholic Church, feelings of victory on the part of young boys, but his mastery of the order of religious life was satisfactory.

And then at thirteen he fell passionately in love with the church. Every sacrament had the heat of blood, every prayer promised eternal damnation. What an extraordinary possibility, he used to think. Eternal damnation. Just the sound of the words on his tongue held a terror and a pleasure for him. He could not bear the excitement of the purity of the virgin—the body and blood of Christ on fire in his mouth. At night under the comforter in the room where he slept next to the girls' room, he held on to himself with a kind of religious ecstasy. He knew, even then he knew, that his love affair with God was carnal. But it went on through university, subdued by reason as he grew older, until Jamey died. Although he knew he would have left the church even if Jamey had lived, he missed in a way too deep for language the daily wonder of belief.

As he lay with his eyes closed in the dark room at Lacey House, he tried to call to mind Jamey's face. He had only two pictures, one at Jamey's christening with Will who had been his godfather holding him up for the camera to see. The second, perhaps the last picture anywhere of Jamey, a blurred picture of a young boy in half profile sitting on the fence outside Mailbones Pub, his collar up against the cold, his chin set in his fists, looking away from the camera down the street toward Marks and Spencer. The face he called to mind was not Jamey's exactly, or if it was he looked very much like the boy Nicholas at the opera and Will wished that the boy were with him, his son, not the child of the unpleasant man in the wheelchair but Will's son, Nicholas Huston, and they were sitting in the dark of the bedroom of Lacey House discussing *Così Fan Tutte* or *Don Giovanni* or football and the weight of his body against Will's arm was wings.

17

Adam didn't move. The blood was streaming across the hardwood floor but in the dim light of the vestibule Annie could not tell when she knelt down beside him from where the blood was coming.

"Adam?" Her hair fell over his shoulders in a tent.

He made no sound. Annie touched his shoulder lightly but he didn't move.

At the top of the stairs, Alexandra appeared in her nightgown. She asked in a voice barely above a whisper, "Mama? Did he fall?"

Annie took a deep breath to still the shaking in her

voice. "He did fall, Lexa, but you should get dressed now and get Nicholas dressed. I'm going to call an ambulance."

Initially, what went through Annie's mind was leaving. She could run upstairs, grab her backpack, dress the children, get a taxi on Connecticut Avenue, and go to R Street. Perhaps there'd be an all-night café or else they'd sit on the front steps of Nora's Restaurant across the street from the house where the priest was staying and wait for him to appear.

It was not compassion she felt kneeling beside her husband, perhaps instinct or a sense of necessity—but she leaned across his body and touched his face, sticky with blood, ran her hand across his forehead, her fingers through his hair. He seemed to flinch, or perhaps the life in his face had not had time to drain out, because she thought—certainly she thought when she looked back later at the events of the evening—that he was dead.

Upstairs, she could hear Alexandra in Nicholas's room. "Hurry, Nich-o," she heard Lexa say. "We have to hurry, fast."

She took Adam's wrist to check his pulse which seemed to her, knowing nothing of pulses, to be strong and fast. As she held his wrist he opened his eyes, turned over on his back, and grabbed her face, covering her mouth with his strong broad hand.

"So, Delirious," he said pulling her face close enough to his to kiss her. "Are you hoping against hope that I am dead?"

Close up, she could see that the blood covering his face seemed to have no source.

She tried to pull away but Adam's upper body was powerful, his hands particularly. He had one hand across her mouth, the arm locking her head, the other arm holding her body, except her legs. She tried to kick the stairs, kick the hardwood floor, but he had pulled her on top of him, his hands now on her throat, his bloodied face against hers. She heard Nicholas beside her, then heard him shout "Hurry up," and then a terrible commotion, a rumbling sound rolling out of Adam from his stomach, and his hands loosened on Annie's throat.

Annie scrambled to her feet.

Beside Adam, Nicholas, dressed in his blue jeans and pajama tops, stood with the skillet which Rebecca had given Annie as a wedding present.

"Shit," Adam shouted, holding his head with both of his hands.

"I hit him," Nicholas said very quietly dropping the skillet on the floor beside him as if it had been the skillet doing the hitting.

Annie took Nicholas's hand and went to the kitchen, turning on the lights as she went. "We need an ambulance," she said to Nicholas keeping his hand in hers. She dialed 911.

"Will he die?" Nicholas asked.

"He'll be fine," Annie said running her hands through his silky hair.

When she went back into the hall, Adam was sitting up, his head in his hands, subdued. Alexandra was standing on the landing.

"I have called an ambulance, Adam," Annie said.

"How thoughtful of you, Delirious," Adam said.

She stayed back from him so he could not take hold of her again if he had that in mind, but he neither moved nor spoke, holding his head in his hands, his eyes closed. When the sound of sirens was clear in the distance, he lay on the floor, face down as he had been when Annie discovered him in the vestibule.

"They're here," Nicholas said quietly.

"They are here," Annie agreed.

And Alexandra from the steps said, "Mama, the ambulance is here."

Two medics arrived, rushing through the front door, kneeling beside Adam. Annie stood in the door to the living room. Her mind was on hold. Adam lay on his back with his eyes closed while the medics checked his pulse, his heart, looked into his ears, lifted the lids of his eyes and checked the pupils with a small flashlight.

One of the medics put on rubber gloves, wiped the blood off Adam's face, and smelled it.

"What happened?" he asked Annie.

"He fell down the stairs," Annie said. "He is in a wheelchair." She indicated the wheelchair still lying on its side behind Adam where it had fallen.

"This is not real blood," the medic said. "I don't

think he's cut himself. I can't see a place where the blood would be coming from.''

''It's stage makeup,'' Alexandra said from the steps. ''He put it on in the bathroom and it's all over the sink.''

''Stage makeup?'' The medic shrugged. ''Sir,'' he said to Adam. ''Are you awake?''

''I have a concussion,'' Adam said in a perfectly clear voice. ''The concussion came from where my son hit me in the head with a frying pan.'' He had opened his eyes. ''That is my son and there on the floor beside you is the frying pan with which he hit me.''

''He was strangling my mother,'' Nicholas said quietly.

The younger medic who had examined Adam stood up and looked at his partner with warning. ''If this is a case of domestic violence, then you should call the police.''

''No,'' Annie said thinly, wishing that her brain would move from a stopped position in her head. ''There was a terrible misunderstanding.''

''What would you like for us to do?'' the older medic asked Annie.

''Marry her,'' Adam said. ''My wife Delirious would very much like it if you would marry her.''

''How badly hurt is he?'' Annie asked.

''Hurt unto death,'' Adam said.

''He seems to be fine,'' the medic said. ''There is a small knot on his head but he was hit in a very hard part of his head and I'd be surprised if there is going to be a concussion. He shows no evidence of anything but made-up blood on his face and he must have had a mouthful of red junk which he spit out on the floor." He indicated the stream of red across the floor of the hall. "Is that correct, sir?" he asked Adam.

"Absolutely correct, sir," Adam said.

"Then you won't take him to the hospital?" Annie said.

"I will if you insist," the medic said. "There just doesn't seem to be a reason to take him. I'll be glad to take you to the police station if you'd like me too, Ma'am, so as you can file a report for domestic violence."

"I don't think so," Annie said. "It's very complicated. Adam was upset."

"Well, sir," the medic asked Adam, "are you less upset now?"

"Do you think you'll be okay at home?" the other medic asked.

"Certainly," Adam said. "I'm splendid, thank you very much, sir, except for a major concussion."

"Then maybe you could take him upstairs to his bedroom," Annie said.

Alexandra slipped down the stairs before the medics carried her father upstairs and waited beside her mother.

"I'd call your family doctor," the one medic said coming down the stairs.

"Would you like us to call the police?" the other medic asked again.

"We'll be fine," Annie said evenly. "Sometimes he gets very upset." She watched them go outside to the ambulance, turn off the flashing lights, and drive away. The telephone rang and it was the O'Donnells next door saying they had seen the ambulance, asking was everything okay. Annie turned on the stove and made hot tea, opened the cookie jar, and passed a chocolate chip cookie to Nich-o and Lexa, eating one herself.

"What's going to happen to me?" Nicholas asked, sitting down at the kitchen table.

"Nothing is going to happen to you, darling," Annie said.

"I could have hurt him."

"You were very brave, Nich-o," Lexa said. "You saved Mama."

"You did, Nich-o," Annie said.

They sat silently at the kitchen table, Nicholas munching on his cookie, pensive but also pleased, Alexandra leaning against Annie with her teacup in her hand, Brunnhilde lying on Annie's lap cleaning her belly.

"So what are we going to do?" Alexandra asked.

"Tomorrow, you and Nich-o are going to Aunt Clementine's for a few days and I will figure out what we will do."

"Will we ever go to Paris?" Nich-o asked, dunking his cookie in his tea.

"I am sure we'll go to Paris," Annie said. "Only tomorrow is not the best time for it."

"Besides," Alexandra said, taking another cookie, "Papa is going to Paris tomorrow."

The living room clock read three A.M. and Annie settled the children on the couch, sitting between them, her feet on the coffee table. They slept soundly, their arms across her belly, while she dozed off and on, conscious of sounds from the bedroom where Adam was.

No one in Washington or Texas knew about Annie's life inside the small, cheerful house on Fessenden Street. Ace had suspected and Sylvie, too, the occasional times that Annie saw her in jail when Sylvie was not concentrated on her own plight, which was fifteen years for armed robbery and as an accomplice in the second-degree murder of a bank teller during which robbery her boyfriend had been killed by a policeman. Sylvie's plight was too much for Annie to assimilate and so she gave no thought to the reason for Sylvie's confinement, concentrating only on the confinement itself.

Which had been her approach to her life with Adam Blakemore. It was her life with him—like her childhood with the Graineys. She lived without complaint because she was not unhappy, even as their estrangement, her sense of danger with him, grew. She simply didn't have the temperament for unhappiness. But she always knew, as she had known as a child, that if the opportunity came to fly, as long as she could keep her children, she would fly.

When she woke with the beginning of dawn, Nicholas

was whispering to her that it was almost six-thirty by the clock in the kitchen and they should pack for Dallas. She woke Alexandra and tiptoed upstairs to pack a small valise.

"Now," Annie whispered after she had checked Adam to determine that he was still sleeping. "You both go downstairs and wait. I'll be right down." She took her green canvas bag from the closet. In the bathroom she packed her toilet articles, a nightgown, several changes of clothes, and dressed quickly in a long blue corduroy dress, high-top shoes, a heavy cardigan. She put on her black beret, pulled it down on her forehead, and tied a purple silk scarf around her neck.

When the ambulance arrived at the accident in Brammel, they took Adam first. She remembered the scene in slow motion as if she had seen it—which she had not because she had kept her eyes closed so she would not have to see Adam. But she heard the conversation—two male voices in particular.

"Take the guy first," one said.

"Easy," another said. "Secure the head."

"The spine," the first medic said. "He may have broken the spine."

"His neck," a third voice said.

"We always secure the head," the second medic said.

"What about the girl?" the first asked.

"Another one's coming," the second said. "Hear it?"

Annie could hear it, the long wail above the sound of cars beating the freeway, still at seventy miles per hour, as if nothing had happened, no red Toyota sailing over the cliff, no lives at risk.

A man knelt down and touched her cheek, put something over her face.

"Easy," he said. "That's just a little oxygen. I think you're going to be fine."

She kept her eyes closed, but filtered light crept under her eyelids and she could see the concrete laces above the freeway, above the place where she was lying.

"Is he going to be okay?" Annie asked.

"Your boyfriend?"

"He's not my boyfriend," Annie said. She reached for something to hold on to. "Is he going to die?"

"I don't think so," the man said.

But Annie kept her eyes shut against the possibility even after the ambulance with Adam had pulled back onto the freeway and turned on its siren.

The plane to Dallas was running ten minutes late. Annie went through security with the children, spoke to the attendant at the Continental desk who assigned them row 13, seats A and B. She found herself memorizing the numbers in her head as if she would need them, as if they were fated to be reproduced in the newspaper the following day. *Continental Flight 31 departing Washington at 8:45 A.M. en route to*

Dallas, Texas, dropped seats A and B in row 13 just over northern Virginia.

Annie took Nicholas on her lap and hid her face in the soft jacket he was wearing. Lexa put her hand on her mother's knee.

"Will you go back home when Nich-o and I leave?" she asked.

"I'll just go back to check on your father and then I have to go to work."

Lexa shook her head.

"Maybe you should just call Papa on the telephone," Alexandra said. "Over there." She pointed to a line of public telephones.

"Maybe," Annie said.

"I think Papa needs a vacation," Nicholas said into the soft cloth of his jacket.

"Promise you won't stay in the house if Papa changes his mind about going to Paris."

"I promise," Annie said, but she had not thought beyond this moment of seeing the children off to Dallas except for following the priest.

At eight thirty-five, when the attendant finally announced that people with small children should board first, Annie walked to the gate. Her children were not small, she thought, but small enough certainly, small enough to disappear or to disintegrate, to lose. The terrible possibilities came on suddenly as payment for her sins with Adam.

"Do we have to go?" Nicholas looked up at his mother.

"It's just for a weekend, Nich-o," Alexandra said. "And Auntie Clem will bake us chocolate cake with jimmies."

"Maybe," Nicholas said. "Only I don't like jimmies."

"When will we come back?" Alexandra asked.

"Sunday night," Annie said taking Lexa's hand, kissing her fingers, almost weeping.

"I will call you the minute you get to Clementine's house," Annie said.

"And you will meet us here when we come back?" Nicholas asked, a sudden shadow of distrust crossing his face.

"Of course," Annie said kneeling to kiss him goodbye. "You know that."

A stewardess came down the long ramp from the plane and held out her hands to them. "Are you the Blakemore children?" she asked.

Annie nodded.

"They are," she said. "Alexandra Blakemore and Nicholas Blakemore," as if their full names spoken would imprint on the world and save them from disaster.

"They'll be fine." The stewardess smiled. "We have pancakes for breakfast," she said walking them down the long corridor away from Annie, who waved gaily when they turned their heads to look at her, gaily, gaily, to give them confidence that the plane would not crash for her sins, that she would be back for them, that their world had constancies and she was one of them.

Outside, the morning sun was bright, the air suddenly cold after the autumn heat wave, and a strong wind was blowing. Annie stood in line for a taxicab.

"3308 Fessenden," she told the driver. "And then I'd like for you to wait because I need to go to Dupont Circle."

The front door of her house on Fessenden was wide open and on the porch Siegfried and Brunnhilde sat together in the sun, licking their paws. She ran up the steps and into the house.

"Adam?" she called.

There was no evidence of a problem although the wind had blown the papers from her desk all over the living room and turned over a vase of yellow freesias on the hall table.

"Adam," she called again and went up the steps. There was no answer and Adam was not in their bedroom. The bed was unmade. His wheelchair was gone. Some of his clothes, mostly shirts, had been thrown on the bottom of the bed and there was a note, on top of his blue-checkered shirt: "Delirious, I have gone to Paris as arranged. Yours, *Adam Thomas Blakemore*."

She went downstairs. There was evidence that he had had breakfast—a banana peel on the kitchen table, a box of raisin bran opened, a milk carton left out of the fridge, and the morning paper opened to the Metro section.

She picked up the telephone and called Gail Blakemore.

When they had married, Gail Blakemore was glad for Annie to take care of Adam, especially after the children were born, but in recent months she had become her son's confidante, engaging in conversations full of amusing secrets which Annie assumed had to do with her.

"Yes." Gail Blakemore answered the phone always with "Yes" as if she were in the middle of conversation.

"It's Annie calling to say that Adam has left the house."

"He is on his way here," Gail Blakemore said in her clipped New England accent. "I understand there is difficulty between you and he has taken a shuttle to New York. I'll meet him there."

"I see," Annie said.

"He said you'd left for work with the children," she said. "That he was writing you a note."

"He did leave me a note," Annie said. She did not mention Paris. "He simply didn't tell me where he was going to be." She hesitated. "I'm worried about Adam," she said.

"There is reason to be concerned about Adam," Gail Blakemore said. "I believe he should stay with us awhile—a week or two."

"Perhaps he should," Annie said. She did not mention what had happened the night before, uneasy with the Blakemores, uncertain of her place. But she did say she thought Adam was troubled. Gail Blakemore hesitated and then she said, without the usual edge of sarcasm to her voice, "He has a troubled mind."

Then Annie called Clementine. She told her about Adam's fall, about the manufactured blood, about his hands around her throat and how Nicholas had hit him, only slightly but enough to surprise him, with Rebecca's iron skillet.

"You have to leave him," Clementine said.

"I am leaving him." Annie caught a glimpse of herself in the long glass on the bathroom door, her face framed by the beret like the face of a medieval Madonna. "That is what I want you to know." She was suddenly out of breath. "I have met someone and there is a chance I am going to Dublin for a few days."

"To Dublin?"

"Dublin, Ireland," Annie said. "I will let you know where I am, Clem, and if by chance I do go, I'll be back in a week so if it's all right for you to keep the children just for this week . . ."

"I never heard a word about this man, Dolores Ann," Clementine said.

"I know," Annie said. "He's very new. Brand new."

"And he's a nice man, not a stranger, is that so?"

Annie laughed lightly. "I think he must be a very nice man," she said. "But I don't really know him, Clem."

"I hope you know him well enough, Dolores Ann," Clementine said, her voice maternal. "There are drug dealers and gang murderers and sex offenders. I read about it all the time. Just yesterday, there were four homicides in Washington, D.C., reported in the Dallas paper."

"I know this man is safe," Annie said. "I absolutely know that."

"Oh sweet Jesus," Clementine said, "I know who he is. He's a priest, isn't he, Dolores Ann? Another one of your Roman Catholic priests."

"Yes," Annie said, "he is a priest."

"Don't do anything foolish," Clementine said. "We already have Athalia dying and Sylvie in jail. I don't think I could manage."

"I won't. I promise," Annie said hanging up the telephone. She took Siegfried and Brunnhilde inside, dumped cat food in their bowl, and as an afterthought ran upstairs to get the red cloth hat she had been wearing the first day she saw the priest in the subway. Then she locked the front door and went down the steps to the waiting taxicab, arriving at Connecticut Avenue just as the priest was hailing a taxi.

18

At the wake, Will had been unable to look at Jamey.

"Say good-bye to him, Will, or you'll never forgive yourself," his mother had said.

It was evening and the family was gathered, drinking and talking and weeping like they did at all of the wakes Will had been to in his life—enough for any life coming as frequently as Christmas, his family going quickly, grandmothers and great-aunts, uncles, even two cousins not much older than he. This wake was no different except the coffin was so small, set on a table in the window of the sitting room, with a vase of flowers at either end and a cross of white carnations at his feet which Bernadette had made since she worked at Dinny's Flower Shop on Angel Street.

"You ought to see him before they close the top, Will," his sister Mary had said to him. "He looks good. They did him natural."

"I can't," Will said leaning against Brendan, their shoulders pressed together. "Later, I'll see."

"He feels too bad," Aunt Bricey, Brendan's mother, in whose arms Jamey had died that afternoon, said. But she kept fussing with him like they all did that evening. Will couldn't even be short with them; they were trying their best to be kind, trying to understand how he was feeling.

The priest came around and said a mass for Jamey, standing by the casket with holy water. Everybody knelt. The girls lined up in front of the tiny casket, Bernadette holding her mother's hand, his father on the horsehair sofa from his grandmother's house, holding his head in his hands, like he'd done for days. Even Brendan got down on his knees and said the Our Father.

But Will could not. He faced the coffin with his hand across his eyes, his head bent as if in prayer so he wouldn't catch a look of Jamey by mistake.

Now in a deep sleep in the darkness of number 11 Lacey House, he was at the wake again, standing while the Our Father was muttered around the room, his hand covering his eyes. Near the end of the prayer, "Forgive us our trespasses as we forgive those who trespass against us," he moved forward toward the casket, dropped his hand from his eyes, gripped the wooden sides, and knelt. When he looked into the coffin at the child lying there with his small hands folded over a crucifix, the boy was not Jamey, not the square-cut black hair, the pale skin of his brother James, but the face of the child Nicholas. He touched the cream-colored porcelain cheek and as he did the boy looked up at him, his lips turned at the corner in a smile.

19

When Annie's taxi arrived on Reservoir Road, the priest was standing in front of the house with dying white petunias. He did not go up the front steps of the house but walked past it, past two other row houses, and then back to a long drive or perhaps an alley into which he disappeared.

Annie waited until she could not see him. Then she paid the driver of her cab and got out.

She walked up the alley, which went past the backs of brick row houses to another street, and halfway there was a left turn past the backs of the houses on Reservoir Road. At the juncture, she saw the priest down the alley on the left standing on a large trashcan, looking into the walled garden of one of the houses. She ducked behind a fence.

The day was cold and glorious with a pure blue sky, a distant sun bright enough to warm her face despite the cold. She looked again.

He was no longer standing on the trashcan but had opened it, looked inside, and closed it without finding anything that he needed apparently. Then she watched him lean forward and peer through a crack in the fence, turn the knob on a garden door although he did not open it. When she looked again, he was headed up the alley and she waited until he was several houses ahead of her to follow.

It was ten-fifteen by her watch. She pulled her beret down on her forehead and walked, fairly slowly since he seemed to be in no hurry, checking as he walked, looking above him, around him, stopping occasionally to look in trashcans, between the cracks of houses, checking the gates to the gardens to see if they were locked perhaps. The alley ended at 34th Street, just before Reservoir Road, and the priest stopped, looking in both directions before he turned right as if he were not certain of his destination. But as he turned he must have seen Annie in the alley, or seemed to see her, because he looked back and then he ran.

It was not easy for Annie to run in her high-top shoes which pinched her toes. She dropped her canvas bag just as she came out to the full sunlight of 34th Street and saw him, running still toward Wisconsin Avenue, saw him turn the corner and disappear.

At Wisconsin, she stopped and looked down the hill.

The priest was at the end of the block buying a newspaper from one of the kiosks and she waited until he slipped into a shop on the corner, the newspaper folded under his arm.

The shop, when she arrived in front of it, was not a shop at all but an Indian restaurant, quite dark and empty, and she could see him through the window flipping through the pages of the newspaper, standing at the counter with a coffee. He saw her too, through the glass, or must have seen her, because he folded the paper and disappeared into a booth in the back of the restaurant.

Will stepped out of the cab on Reservoir Road into the bright morning sun, lightened in spirit by the day. The Maguires had left, or at least Michael had. His car was not in front of the house. Will walked close enough to the house to see the front window, the shadow of a person passing by the living room, perhaps Priscilla, perhaps a cleaning person. Then he went back down the street to the alley, turning left behind the Maguires' house, number seven from the corner. He counted. The back gates were wooden with handles, and he turned the handle of the Maguires' but it was locked. Along the alley, large green trashcans on wheels were lined neatly beside the back gates, so he stood on the one marked in large black numbers 3524 Reservoir and looked in the back garden. The kitchen door opened onto a small porch, as did the doors, two of them, to the dining room. There were stairs down from the porch to the brick patio, lined with plastic containers for plants, now empty, several planters with evergreens, and a small wrought iron table with two chairs. On the back of the house, just under the second-story windows, he counted the spotlights, three of them, which would light the patio in the dark. So he could leave by the kitchen door, should Priscilla arrive while he was still with Michael tonight. Or after he had killed him. After he had killed him —the words slipped easily across his brain. He had been writing plays too long for the actual reality of this journey in pursuit of Michael Maguire to unsettle him. So, he decided, he would leave by the kitchen door, run across the patio which would be sufficiently lit for him to see where he was going, and either climb over the fence to the alley or go through the gate if it was possible to open from the inside. He climbed off the trashcan and lifted the lid to determine whether he should get rid of his cassock and the gun immediately, if he should stop long enough to disrobe and wrap the gun. The trashcan was half full of green plastic bags with ties, and by night he ought to be able to see by the floodlights on the Maguires' house.

At the end of the alley which opened to 34th Street, he looked back. There was a woman behind him—not very far behind him and walking at a clip. Priscilla Maguire? Could it be Priscilla Maguire in a long blue dress after him with such purpose? Had she spotted him when he stood on the trashcan? he wondered. He began to run, down 34th

Street, up a small street onto Wisconsin Avenue. At a kiosk, he bought the *Washington Post* and went into an Indian restaurant just beyond the kiosk.

The restaurant was empty except for one waiter who served him a demitasse black coffee while he stood at the counter reading the newspaper under a dim light.

The notice was on page 14 of the Metro section—a small notice but quite accurate to his memory:

PRIEST TAKES GUN FROM
SILVER SPRING SHOP

A priest entered a gun shop on Georgia Avenue, Silver Spring and robbed Marion Webb, age 57, owner of GUNS: NEW AND OLD, of a .38 revolver with a single round of cartridges. By the time the police appeared, the priest had escaped. The owner of the gun shop was unharmed.

Will folded the Metro section and when he looked up a woman, perhaps the one he had noticed in the alley, perhaps Priscilla Maguire, was on the other side of the window of the restaurant. He took the newspaper and went into a booth with high wooden sides in the back of the restaurant. He knew he was being followed.

It occurred to him that Priscilla Maguire, a straightforward, unimaginative, and reasonable woman, was not the sort of person to follow anyone. She didn't seem to have an interest in dramatic possibilities. If she had looked out her back window and seen a priest, even a familiar one, standing on her trashcan, looking into her backyard, then she would have been more likely to open the window to ask him directly what he was doing than to follow him.

He finished reading, folded the paper, and stood up, checking the front window. Outside, the woman had disappeared, and even if she had been there he wondered if he would have recognized her since he could not remember whether her hair was blond or brown, too preoccupied was he with the matters of the moment.

He hailed a cab.

"Catholic University," he said.

It seemed appropriate to Will Huston to spend his last day as a priest in the company of friends, his last hours pure in the eyes of God before the meeting which would most certainly change his life for good.

20

The priest got out of the taxi at the entrance to Catholic University and crossed the campus, walking with a sense of purpose, nodding as he passed a group of priests who were coming through the glass doors of the student union. When Annie, out of breath from running in the clear, cold morning air, dashed through the doors after him, the priest was already across the hallway in front of her, standing in line in the cafeteria with coffee and orange juice and two muffins on his tray.

He sat at a table in the corner of the room and took out what appeared to be, from the table where Annie sat down, a turquoise blue Penquin edition of a Shakespeare play. That pleased her. She loved Shakespeare. She especially loved to act in the lighthearted comedies of mistaken identities, his plays of disguises.

Annie was thirteen the summer she started to wear disguises. She remembered that summer in particular because it was unbearably hot. The house in Brammel was empty except for Annie and Billy Joe—Sylvie was fifteen, pregnant and without a husband, living in Houston with Rebecca's sister until the baby was born and given away; Richie was eighteen, working in a filling station; Tom Boy was nineteen in the service; Athalia was married to Big Bill, a Baptist minister whose mind according to Ace was small enough to fit into the shell of a peanut. Sambo had joined a religious cult in California and sent the family prayers written on the backs of postcards, and Clementine was married to a respectable Mexican man and lived in a house with curtains and Spanish reproduction furniture, even a piano in the living room.

Annie loved her family; she simply didn't want to be like them. So their absence the summer of her thirteenth year was unbearably sad, especially on the long hot days without air conditioning. She would sit on her bed in the room under the dormers which she had shared with Clementine and Athalia and Sylvie, the air still as death, and weep into her full cotton skirt.

It was the summer that Annie became an actress in her heart, surviving the tedium and loneliness, the long days of Rebecca's carping, Ace's drinking, by dressing up. In disguise, she could fly out of the house.

"You're going crazy if you keep this up, Dolores Ann," Rebecca said one afternoon, so hot the ice for the lemonade melted before it got to the glass. "You won't know who you are."

"I am who you see," Annie said sitting at the kitchen table, her hair under a baseball cap, dressed in Richie's Little League uniform, freckles sprinkled with makeup across her nose. "My voice is changing."

"Dolores Ann is dumb," Billy Joe said from the floor where he was arranging his baseball cards. "Don't you think Dolores Ann is dumb, Mama?"

"I think Dolores Ann is going crazy," Rebecca said.

Ace was lying in the window seat, his feet propped up on the wall, sleeping off his bourbon, his eyes closed, but he was sober enough to hear the conversation.

"Leave Dolores Ann alone, Rebecca," he said. "It's hard to be a thirteen-year-old boy when you didn't make first string on the Little League team. You don't know about being a boy."

"The dreaming Dolores Ann does instead of Christian service comes from you, Ace," Rebecca said. "And look where it got you."

"No comment," Ace said.

"Of course you don't have a comment," Rebecca said. "You're too drunk for commenting."

"Thank you, Papa," Annie said later to Ace.

"Don't thank me, chicken soup," Ace said. "Thank your own sweet dreams to save your life."

Will Houston put *Hamlet* down and stared across the room at nothing in particular—a young girl with curly black hair who resembled Maud with her plate-round face, the clock over the door which read half past eleven, a tall, hefty, athletic-looking boy in running clothes who had just come through the door. His eyes couldn't settle, his mind darted from one thought to another—Hamlet played by Judith Anderson in the forties perhaps, the broken chandelier at the Abbey and whether it would fall on the heads of an unsuspecting audience, why Americans didn't have a convivial place to sit for coffee at theaters instead of standing overdressed, drinking wine from plastic glasses in lobbies kept too cold for comfort. Perhaps they sold chocolate-covered peanuts at this cafeteria. He thought about the boy Nicholas with a sudden sadness, knowing he would not see him again.

And then he saw the woman in a black beret staring off into the middle distance, who must be—he was certain of it—the same woman he had seen the day before wearing a brown broad-brimmed hat and looking for counsel from a priest.

Will Huston put *Hamlet* in his trouser pocket and walked through the cafeteria, noisy with the agreeable laughter of students, and across the hall to the men's.

Annie waited. She moved to a table just across from the men's room so she would not miss him, her chin resting on her folded hands so as not to fall asleep. At noon she called the opera company to say she was ill and would be out for a day or two. She took out her compact and rubbed her cheeks pink. She looked tired.

She did not think about the unlikelihood of her situation, but a kind of unreality had taken over since the children left for Dallas. She had scenes in mind, one in which the priest took her in his arms at Gate A just as the flight to Dublin was boarding and said he would stay in America, stay with her forever. There was a scene in a small village church in Ireland where she was wearing a white Victorian dress, her hair woven with daisies.

She could see herself running across the Dulles International Airport. He had her by the shoulders. They were standing next to the ticket counter in view of the other passengers.

"Bless you, child," he was saying to her. Annie loved that. Bless you, child. She could feel in her blood the forgiveness those words of his would bring.

And sometime between that moment of imagining and twelve thirty-four by the clock over the door to the cafeteria, Annie fell asleep.

21

On the subway from Brookland to Union Station, empty except for a sleepy policeman who leaned against the rail by handicapped seating, it occurred to Will that a policeman, like this one, might be looking for a priest who met his description. The woman in the black beret could have made a report. Will opened the Metro section of the November 21, 1991, *Washington Post* and settled behind it in case the officer recalled a description registered at police headquarters of a gray-haired priest, about five foot eleven, with olive complexion and green-flecked eyes. The gentleman in the gun shop had seemed to be the sort of man attentive to small details—but then, of course, he had left the gun on

"Union Station," the policeman said. "Straight ahead from the station," he said. "You can't miss it."

The train had stopped between stations and Will was uncomfortable standing next to the policeman as if in such close proximity they should be engaging in conversation.

"It's awful about that boy killed yesterday," Will said without thinking, not planning to say anything more to the policeman, certainly not about the boy.

"What boy?" the policeman asked, his eyes open now, his arms folded across his chest.

"The boy hit by the bus."

"Northeast?"

"I don't know the city well," Will said. "It said Pinehurst Circle in the paper."

"Northwest," the policeman said solemnly. "One was hit in the northeast as well."

"By a bus?"

"I can't remember."

"Two children killed in a day in a small city," Will said. "It makes you sick."

"This is a dangerous city for children," the policeman said. "I have two boys myself. I'd move if I could."

The train started up again, moving slowly into the lights of Union Station.

"Your stop, Father," the policeman said to Will and he touched Will's arm just slightly, behind the elbow, but it was a gesture which brought a flood of sweet feelings.

"Thank you, officer," Will said giving a half wave as the doors to the subway were closing.

He went up the escalator to the daylight of 1st Street, his blood warm in his veins, his feelings running too high for the duties of this day.

In the station he called Brendan, knowing his cousin would be out, leaving a message on his answering machine.

"Hello Bren," he said. "I'll be coming in tonight but quite late. I'll give you a call when I know the time so you can arrange to let me in the flat."

As he walked across the station toward the Visitors Center, his eye caught a small dark-haired woman in a hat and he was alarmed. But on second glance, it wasn't the woman he had seen earlier in the cafeteria of Catholic University. He stopped to check if he was being followed, although certainly the woman in hats had not seen him leave the men's room at the university. She had been resting, her head turned away from him, and several times on his way to Brookland station he had looked around to check. She could not anticipate his whereabouts now even if she were following him—if it were not simply a coincidence that they happened to be in the same place again and again.

It was one forty-five. Four and a half hours to Michael Maguire. Four and a half hours to tea and crumpets with Mikey Maguire—to sherry with Secretary Maguire.

"I beg your pardon," he said to the woman behind

the counter at the Visitors Center. "Where is the best gallery for pictures nearby?"

"What kind of pictures do you want to see?" she asked him.

"Any pictures," Will said. "But I like a gallery which is pleasant and not too dark with a place for tea nearby."

The woman looked at her watch.

"There's the 1492 exhibition in the East Wing of the National Gallery," she said. "It's the biggest we've ever had at the gallery, so it said in the paper."

"Can I walk from here?"

"No problem," the woman said. She took out a map and drew the route in orange marker. "Ten minutes to the East Wing, maybe fifteen." She handed him the map. "And there's a cafeteria below."

Will bought a pack of cigarettes and walked out of Union Station, past a well-dressed man on crutches who stopped him to ask with exaggerated politeness if he had money for food. Will gave him a dollar and walked past a long line of people waiting for taxicabs. The dark-haired woman in the hat was in line, kissing a man about her height in a ski cap who appeared, perhaps by his dress, to be much younger than she was. Will actually stopped to look at their kissing, titillated by it, although up close the woman was not the kind of woman who appealed to him. How long since he'd been with a woman? he wondered. Not since summer certainly, except for kissing Molly Kelly when she played Millicent to his Jim Canary in *Baleful Lover*—running his hands down her panties a little drunk after the cast party and wanting her then in the costume closet where they'd ducked for a moment. But Molly was married to a barrister with two children and Will had gotten old enough not to push desire every single time it announced itself. To let the moment go. He hadn't actually been with a woman since he stayed with Mara off and on for several months last year. And then when the news of Michael Maguire's reappearance was in the *Belfast Times,* he lost interest in love affairs.

He walked away from the station, down the wide tree-lined street toward the Capitol. There was a new shadow over the day; the light had a peppered quality as if a photograph had been poorly developed; the sidewalks were empty. At Constitution Avenue he followed the orange line on his map and turned right, keeping the Capitol behind him. It was quite a fine-looking Capitol building, he thought, and the avenue was lovely and broad, lined with large white buildings carefully landscaped. But there was an anonymity about the streets, a lack of character, although the city looked like Paris, was certainly as beautiful as Paris. Will had no sense of being anywhere—no scents, no smell of burning chestnuts on the streets which was the smell of cities he knew in the autumn months, no voices in animation rising above the traffic. An occasional well-dressed man or woman with an umbrella or briefcase, but no life to speak of on the sidewalk in this city that was at the center of the Western world—as though it were all an invention of the late twentieth century. "We are such stuff as dreams are made of and our poor lives are rounded by a sleep"— he liked the way the iambic pentameter slipped across his tongue, fleshy as ripe peaches.

He crossed the avenue, zigzagging through a maze of traffic to the East Wing, a slice of white marble and slender glass on the corner of Constitution Avenue and 4th.

The line for the 1492 exhibition was extremely long, but he waited nevertheless behind a young man with an unwashed ponytail who was sleeping on his feet and had to be tapped on the shoulder whenever it was time to move forward in line. Will needed a conversation to quiet his growing anxiety, his stomach in turmoil, his palms perspiring, very like the feelings he had when the theater was dark, just before the lights went up, and he was onstage, maybe ready with his first line or maybe his mind had flattened.

There was a tap on Will's arm and he turned to face a young woman, a mass of beige curls to her shoulders and smelling strongly of gardenia.

"The line has moved up," she said softly and then laughed. "I thought you were sleeping on your feet."

"Oh no," Will said, although he did suddenly feel as if he had lost time. "No, wide awake. It's the gentleman in front of me sleeping on his feet."

The man with the ponytail looked at Will straight on

and though his voice was quiet there was no doubt about his state of mind. "I don't like remarks made by strangers, Father," he said.

Will nodded.

When he looked back, the girl with the beige hair was rolling her eyes and he smiled at her. She seemed familiar to him as well. Was everyone familiar? he thought. Had the world become so small that women could be repeated and repeated in a single day, or was it that his imagination could only accommodate a few women and so he imposed the presence of those few on all the women he saw? With this woman, it was not the gardenia smell of her which was familiar but something about her small, precise features or maybe it was the mass of curly hair.

"Is this your first time at the exhibit?" she asked.

Will nodded.

"It's extensive, you know. I've been back twice already."

"I didn't know it was long."

"Very."

Will looked at his watch. "Perhaps I ought to come back tomorrow," he said. He didn't want to be caught in a long line, certainly not behind the unpleasant man with the ponytail, and so he smiled at the beige-haired woman, walked across the bright main gallery floor, and inquired of the guard the way to the cafeteria which, he discovered, could be got to beneath the street on the kind of walking conveyor he'd seen in airports.

Along one glass wall was a waterfall, or more exactly a wall of running water, altogether agreeable, he thought, taking a seat next to it with his tray of tea and biscuits.

It was not even three o'clock and although he might eat his tea and biscuits slowly, there was still too much time to wander through before evening. He had to keep his nerves from taking over as they could do, had done in the past in daily life, in matters like his father's death or Bernadette's appendicitis or even the labored two-step back and forth with Maud in the days before they stopped trying to have a love affair. But onstage, no matter his anxiety, he had never bungled in a play, lost a line or two of course, forgotten his place, but his instinct for the heart of the play was so true that he knew what ought to happen in the course of action even if he had lost the precise way the playwright had written it. Daily life was a different matter and this afternoon was daily life. In extremis, perhaps but true nevertheless.

Daily Life: In Extremis, he thought. *An Irish Comedy.* But he had lost the energy for writing plays this afternoon— and was just beginning to plan what he would think about, order his mind to travel down a linear path, when the beige-haired girl who had been standing behind him in the line to the 1492 exhibition came off the conveyor from the East Wing and walked along the wall of water toward his table.

"You dropped this," she said holding out the map.

"You left your place in line to bring this to me?" Will

took the map of Washington, D.C., with the orange line from Union Station to the National Gallery of Art.

"My boyfriend kept my place," the girl said. "But I worried you might get lost without this map. And then what?"

She smiled at him, a lovely smile which lit her face.

"Then what indeed?" he said. "That was very kind of you."

She gave a small curtsy.

"I'm Irish," she smiled. "Three quarters. I thought if I were good to you, you might bring me luck."

"I hope I do," Will said. And he blew her a kiss.

Immediately, he knew the wrongness of the gesture—not something Father James would do—not a priestly gesture at all, certainly not from this wry and quiet priest preparing for revenge in whose robes he had spent two days. The girl, however, had not noticed a slip in character, too taken was she with the grace from good deeds, the chance for good luck perhaps. She giggled and waved back, rushing after her boyfriend in line for 1492.

Will was pleased to have the map, disoriented as he had sometimes felt in Washington, and he spread it out on the round table to study. What he really needed, he decided, was his own uncomplicated map with the places he had been, so he took a napkin from the dispenser and copying from the city map drew his own to fill the time.

Later in the main gallery, he bought several postcards of the Dutch masters, for no particular reason except it seemed the normal thing to do after a visit to a gallery and he did like the richness of the paint on canvas of the Dutch, the reproduction of those fleshy faces in their squarish hats, staring straight out at the viewer.

Outside a wind was picking up, the sky was very gray, the sense of rain coming, and the air felt good on his face, a familiar Dublin cold. Perhaps he should walk back to Lacey House, he thought, and asked a policeman on the corner of 7th and Constitution how far to Dupont Circle by foot.

"Thirty minutes walking fast," the policeman said without hesitation. "Down to 17th and turn right straight to the Circle."

At Dupont Circle, he'd have a drink. One scotch to make the blood burn, not enough to numb the senses. He had to stop by Lacey House and leave a note to check out, which meant that Father John might be there so he must allow time for conversation, not to leave the poor man hanging altogether. He planned to say that he had an emergency in Eugene, Oregon, where some members of his family lived, and therefore would have to leave before he had anticipated. He liked the name Eugene and imagined the coast of Oregon would be a place to his liking, like Ireland, with high drama and a sense of danger from the ferocious Pacific Ocean. But he did not know whether Eugene was on the coast. He'd make arrangements with Father John to meet for a late dinner; he felt particularly chagrined about Father John as if, as happened when a man is burdened with another man's story, he had a responsibility for the way things would work out.

At Le Potage, a small French café on 17th Street, he took a table by the window and ordered a scotch.

There was a pretty girl sitting at the counter with her baby strapped across her chest, its small head against her arm, and Will was touched to see her there, drinking something in a mug, nibbling a cracker.

He took out a postcard of a Hans Holbein vicar with ruddy cheeks and olive eyes, turned it to the back. Starting at the top he began a list of the women in his life since Jamey's death. Before Jamey, there had only been Mary Hozier, called Virgin Mary Hozier, Mary mother of God, by his sisters although he used to kiss her in the back closet of her mother's house until he thought he'd die of it, rubbing himself up against the wall since Mary Hozier wouldn't allow him against her covered thighs.

Maeve MacIntire was the first woman on the list.

Maeve MacIntire. Irish. (He wrote them as if they were a record of death.) 1971–1973, off and on.

Teresa Zawaki (Polish actress). September–December 1977.

Sarah Thomas (Irish). Married May 2, 1978. Annulled without issue September 1984.

Bernice Mallory (Irish). 1981–1983. Stillborn daughter born August 11, 1981, baptized Helen, buried at St. Peter's RC Church, Dublin.

Sally LeFevre (American actress). February–June 1985.

Maud O'Connor (Irish). 1984–1991.

Sally LeFevre: 1986 tour in States
                1989 tour in States
                1990 tour in States

He finished the scotch, put the Holbein postcard in his pocket, and paid. The pretty girl was getting ready to leave and he thought to wait for her, to strike up a conversation, especially when she smiled at him, a small shy smile which barely turned the corners of her lips. Then he could put her last on the list, with the girl at the gallery. So little he knew the women who had passed through his life—like roles he remembered, what it was like to be Uncle Vanya or Mercutio, like the taste of beer or the look on a woman's face against the pillow but briefly, briefly. Nothing which took hold of his heart and demanded that he lay claim.

When Will arrived, Father John was sitting in the parlor at Lacey House reading the *Washington Post* but he put down the paper immediately.

"Father James," he called, getting to his feet.

"Hello, Father," Will said checking his watch. It was four forty-five, which gave him only thirty minutes. "I was hoping to catch you before I met my friends for drinks."

"Well, here I am," Father John said. "There was a woman by to see you half an hour ago."

"A woman?" They walked up the stairs together and Will, suddenly out of breath with this news, leaned into Father John speaking softly. "Unlike you, Father, I know no women except my dear mother."

Father John shrugged.

"Well, she knew you by description at least. 'Gray hair and a reddish scar just so,' she said. She's a very pretty woman with black hair and high cheekbones, exceptionally nice skin, I thought to myself, and such small hands. She says her name is Annie Blakemore."

"Annie Blakemore?"

"That's what she said."

"Very strange," Will said, certain with a terrible sinking that it was the woman in the black beret. He opened the door to his room. "I honestly don't know an Annie Blakemore," he said.

"I told her we'd be having dinner round about eight if she was really desperate to be in touch with you today. And she said in fact, she was a bit desperate and would be back then." Father John smiled. "Very pretty, Father. You shouldn't have been a priest."

"Well, life is long enough for changes, Father," Will said. "See you later, about eight in the parlor."

Will sat down on the end of his bed, breathing deeply. He should not have had the scotch.

Annie Blakemore, he thought to himself. Annie Blakemore. He didn't know an Annie Blakemore in Dublin and certainly he knew no one in America except Brendan's doltish American wife and Sally LeFevre, so either the woman at the 1492 exhibition had followed him or it was the girl in the hat. He went over the list of associations he had made in his two days in Washington. It occurred to him that of course it could have to do with the stealing of the gun and Annie Blakemore could be the shopkeeper's wife or his daughter or a plainclothes detective hired by the police department of Washington, D.C., to track him down.

22

Annie woke with a start and for a moment she forgot where she was, in a roomful of unfamiliar people, or even who she was, her face sticky with makeup, the print of pale lipstick on her hand where she had fallen asleep.

The priest was gone.

She had not noticed the time before she fell asleep but by the clock on the wall of the cafeteria it was now one-fifteen. Certainly she couldn't have slept long—dozed, perhaps, for a few minutes after a night of sitting up on the couch in the living room alert to Adam on the second floor. No wonder she was exhausted. She took off her beret, brushed her hair with her hands, and wiped the makeup off her hand. Then she pulled the beret down so it covered her head to just above the eyes.

At one-thirty, Annie called Clementine who was off with Lexa and Nich-o to take a chocolate cake and perfume to Sylvie.

"Lilac, Alexandra says, is Sylvie's favorite," Clementine said.

Alexandra got on the phone, her voice full of excitement. "Aunt Clem says maybe, maybe Sylvie will be out of jail by Christmas and today, if we get there by two, we might get to see Ice Pick Brittle who has a black patch over one eye because it got ruined in an ice pick fight."

Nicholas told Annie that he didn't want to see Ice Pick but he liked the way the police guard stood in the room with his arms folded across his chest when they visited jail. "Remember?" Nich-o asked.

"Aunt Clem says maybe you will let us stay the whole week and miss school since already I'm ahead of a lot of people in my class and Nich-o only reads books in school and doesn't do his math whether he's there or not," Lexa said.

"Maybe," Annie said. "If it's okay with Clem."

"And if you're not too lonely," Alexandra said. "Did Papa go to Paris?"

"He's gone to Connecticut to visit your grandparents," Annie said.

"Well, Mama, if you have to stay alone tonight, sleep

with Siegfried and lock your doors," Lexa said. "Hugs and kisses."

"Hugs and kisses," Nicholas said.

"Now, Dolores Ann," Clementine said lowering her voice to a whisper. "You are not going after trouble, are you?"

"No, Clemmie," Annie said. "Trust me. I know exactly what I'm doing. I'll call you tonight."

The row houses across the street from Lacey House were gray and misty in the light rain. Annie sat on a bottom step opposite, down a few houses toward 20th, just far enough away not to be noticed by the priest when he arrived. The steps were not yet wet but cold through her skirt and she pulled her knees up, her hat down on her brow to conceal her face.

For a long time, she waited watching the afternoon fade to dusk, but no one came at all until shortly after four o'clock when a taxicab pulled up to the house on R Street. An unfamiliar priest got out of the taxi, paid the driver, went up the steps, and opened the front door, which seemed to be unlocked. When Annie knocked several minutes later, he was the one who answered the door.

"I wonder if you know a priest from Dublin who was staying here," she asked. "A gray-haired priest with a scar across his cheek."

"Indeed," the priest who answered the door said. "I'll be having dinner with him this evening."

"Perhaps you could give him a message then," Annie said. "Tell him that Annie Blakemore came by to see him."

"He'll be back by six, I'm sure," the priest said. "If you'd like to stop by again."

"I would," Annie said. "It's sort of an emergency."

"I'll tell him that you came by." The priest smiled. "A lovely woman called Annie Blakemore, I'll say. With very small hands."

Just after she settled herself once again on the steps across the street, another priest left the house, one she had not seen. He turned toward Connecticut Avenue, stopping to pick a rose geranium in a pot by the front steps, put the flower in the top button of his cassock, and Annie was struck by the unlikely gesture.

In the hospital room of St. Francis Xavier where she had been taken after the accident, there had been rose geraniums. She remembered the smell in particular, which had been too strong, and she had asked Clementine to remove the flowers from her bedside table and put them in the window across from her bed.

The priest in residence at St. Francis Xavier had come in during the first few days saying a prayer next to her bed, taking her hand while he spoke in Latin. But it wasn't until the third day after the accident that Annie had spoken to him, having been until then in a state of semiconsciousness.

He was quite an old priest, as she remembered, but his eyes were a wonderful bright blue and his voice was large and low, his manner slow, the way he put his hand on her forehead or touched her shoulder. She had not been badly hurt in the accident, bruised and cut with mild internal bleeding and shock, but the doctors kept her in the hospital because she seemed disoriented and unnaturally silent. She showed few signs of recovery and although her brain scan gave no evidence of head injury, the doctors were concerned that something neurological might materialize. Adam, she knew, was badly injured and had been moved to another hospital in downtown Dallas which had a shock trauma unit. She did not know that he had been paralyzed in the accident or even, for certain, that he was alive. Rebecca wanted Annie moved to the same hospital with Adam, maintaining that the medical attention was more professional, although as Ace told Annie it was actually the Catholics that disturbed Rebecca, not the standards of medical practice at St. Francis Xavier. Annie was glad to stay at St. Francis. She didn't wish to be at a hospital with Adam although she made no effort to communicate that with her family, keeping her eyes closed most of the time, unresponsive when people spoke to her.

But on the third day when the priest came and stood beside her bed, Annie wanted to talk.

"I need to make a confession," she said to the priest. She folded her hands under her chin. "Forgive me, Father, for I have sinned," she said quietly into her hands and she could feel the priest lean over her to hear her more clearly although her eyes were closed. "I was driving Adam's car that he got from his father for graduation," she said. "It was a red Toyota and I was driving him to the Dallas airport so he could go back to New York to his fine and fancy life because he discovered when he came to Brammel that my family was not like his—white trash is what he thought we were, so Sylvie says."

The priest pulled up a chair and sat down.

"So I hated him for that." She held her hands over her eyes so she did not have to see the priest's response. "And I was so angry I started to drive faster and faster and there was a blue truck going along and Adam was saying go slower and I was instead going faster because of how angry I was and then—that's all," she said. "We crashed. I don't even remember any noise."

The priest gave her prayers to say, thanking Jesus and the Blessed Mother for her life, and a prayer for the recovery of Adam. And then he was gone.

Annie had wanted for him to forgive her, to take her in his arms, lift her from the bed, fly with her over the trees so she did not feel the great weight of her own body.

"It was a terrible accident," she had wanted him to say. "But only an accident."

She called to him but he had left. She even put her light on for the nurse, who said the priest was in Mrs. Cruise's room and would Annie like him back for any reason and she said no.

Annie had stayed in the hospital for a week but the priest to whom she had confessed did not come back. Another priest, a breezy and outgoing young man who seemed to take his duties lightly, came by, getting her name wrong although it was written on the chart on the door, calling her Sally, staying briefly, only time to recite a quick prayer and to tell an Irish joke.

Falling in and out of sleep during the days at St. Francis Xavier, she dreamed about the old blue-eyed priest, listened to his deep voice playing in her mind. She seldom thought of Adam although she did go over the details of the accident, as much as she could remember. Clementine told her that Adam was not great—as she put it—that he was going to have some trouble learning to walk, and Athalia told her that his neck was broken in two and he would never walk again.

"I wonder if you could find out for me what happened to that priest who came to see me the first days and hasn't been back," Annie asked Sylvie the day before she was to be discharged. "He was quite old but he had wonderful shiny blue eyes."

"Mama told me about him," Sylvie said. "I'll ask what's come of him."

Sylvie found out that night from one of the nurses at the nurses' station.

"So?" Annie asked.

"He died," Sylvie said.

"He died?"

"He died on Tuesday night," Sylvie said. "That's what the nurse said."

"He was here Tuesday," Annie said. "He talked to me." She put her arm over her eyes. "I can't believe it, Sylvie," she said. "I told him everything."

"He wasn't one of your priests, was he, Dolores Ann?" Sylvie asked.

"I expected him to come back the next day and tell me it was not my fault," Annie said.

"But it wasn't your fault," Sylvie said brushing the hair off Annie's forehead. "It was an accident. That's what the word accident means."

"No, Sylvie," Annie said. "The word accident means terrible things."

From her step on R Street, Annie could see the priest walking a block down toward 2115 and she turned away, pulled her beret down, opened a copy of *Così Fan Tutte,* and pretended to read. But her face was hot with excitement.

"I am Annie Blakemore," she would say to him. "Remember? We met two days ago in the subway. Remember my red hat?"

Once, she started to cross the street after she had seen him go inside the house but she lost her nerve and sat back down on the steps with *Così Fan Tutte* in her lap.

There was a sharp chill in the air, the coming of dark. Lights went on in two of the upstairs rooms of Lacey House and she saw a man with a newspaper under his arm in one of the rooms.

Annie had not thought about her hands as small before, although there used to be talk about Ace's hands amongst the girls and she remembered one afternoon on the roof, Sylvie smoking, probably even drinking whiskey as she took to doing in high school, Athalia disapproving but vigilant, Clemmie probably married by then.

"Look at those little hands you got, Dolores Ann," Sylvie said. "Like Papa's."

"And won't do a lick of work either in the eyes of God," Athalia said.

"Dolores Ann's been painting cars in the body shop with those small hands," Sylvie said.

"I said in the eyes of God," Athalia said.

Annie looked down now at her hands and wondered at the look of her in her black beret and long blue dress. What would the priest see were he to look at her? Would he see a pretty woman in a black beret or would he notice the brightness of her eyes, her high cheekbones? Would he see her as she wished to see herself—a small, brave, brightly colored creature with wings clipped to fly just over the high grasses and under the branches of the trees? Or was the heart of Annie Blakemore forever in disguise?

Just then, a taxicab pulled up in front of Lacey House and the priest rushed out the door and climbed in the backseat.

23

Will was surprised at how well he felt, almost at ease, as he walked up the front steps of the Maguires' house on Reservoir Road, the evening luminous with streetlights, the damp air familiar. He snapped a dead petunia off the spread of plants in the window boxes and dropped it in the bushes.

There was a moment backstage, just before the curtain went up on a new play on opening night, when a sudden calm came over Will, a sense of stillness—when he became at his marrow the character he was meant to be, as if the transformation from himself to someone else was only possible at the moment of absolute necessity.

He rang the bell.

·   ·   ·

In his bedroom at Lacey House, he had dressed for the last time as Father James Grady. He put the Playbills and copies of the *Washington Post,* the empty boxes of chocolate-covered peanuts, a pack of cigarettes in the wastebasket, pulled up the covers of his bed, checked himself in the mirror without his wig, shaking out the wig and brushing the stiff gray hair in the front with his fingers. Then he wrote two notes, one to Father John Holloman which said: "A family emergency calls me out of town. I wish you good luck." He added, although it seemed out of character even for Father James Grady, "You are in my prayers. Until we meet again."

The second note he left on his bed, deciding at the last minute against checking out of Lacey House in person, avoiding the questions which might arise. "Family Emergency. $44.00 for three nights plus tip. Gratefully yours, Father James Grady." He left a fifty-dollar bill on top of the bed sheets.

He checked the gun, checked how quickly it would take to pull it out of his pocket, to cock it, to shoot, going over and over the procedure in his mind.

No one seemed to be at home. He rang the bell again. Then he heard a voice call "Coming" and footsteps in the hall behind the door, a small commotion.

The front door opened and Michael Maguire, diminished by the years, pale, flaccid, a bit vacant in the eyes as if he had not been equal in character to the process of daily living, stood close enough to touch.

The weakness of Michael's appearance enraged Will now. He had a soft, washed-out kind of look which Will remembered from cowardly boys on the streets of Belfast who played on fragile lives, torturing the cats in the neighborhood, the smaller children, the girls.

"Michael Maguire." Will extended his hand. "I'm Jamey Grady from Belfast."

Michael Maguire, perplexed, stood aside and ushered Will in.

"Remember me?" Will asked.

"Well, I'm awfully pleased to see you, Father, but in truth I don't remember," he said.

"You don't?" Will said jovially. "I certainly didn't think you were so drunk as to forget the summer of 1969 when we were buddies."

He followed Michael Maguire into the living room, which had been prepared for his arrival with a delft blue dish of yellow goldfish crackers on the coffee table, three wine glasses, a bottle of red wine, and a bottle of whiskey half empty in a room which was otherwise impeccably neat.

"Please sit down." Michael Maguire gestured to a wing chair and folded himself into the down of a large white couch. He examined the cushion of the seat next to him, brushing it with his hand, looking at his hand under the lamplight, although the cushion appeared spotless.

"We have a cat," he said. "My wife's cat."

"I met your wife yesterday," Will said. "But unfortunately, not her cat."

"Yes," Michael Maguire said. "Well, she ought to be home any moment—round about six-thirty, she said." He laughed, not a particularly easy laugh. "She's punctilious, is Priscilla."

Will checked his watch. Three minutes after six, and if Priscilla was punctual as well she would arrive just after Michael Maguire had died.

If not, if she came early, would he invent a story? Or would he tell her the truth and would she understand the white fury of revenge?

Revenge. Maud had looked the word up in the *Oxford* one evening maybe three years past for they still were sleeping in the same bed—Will not sleeping and Maud annoyed at the way the bed and coverlets moved back and forth all night, keeping her restless with him.

"I can't do anything about it," Will had said. "I can't retaliate and so I can't sleep."

"Well, it's going on for too long, almost seventeen years, and I'm not willing to die this slow death with you, Will Huston, so you'll have to find some revenge and clear your system of this poison. Maybe you should write a play."

"A play called *Revenge.*" He had turned on the lamp next to the bed and Maud got up to look at the dictionary on his desk across the room.

"Revenge," she said. " 'To inflict punishment or exact

retribution for . . . The brother of the deceased took up arms to revenge him,' " she read. "It has it right here in the *Oxford* so it must be a common circumstance, brothers being wronged." She read on. " 'Revenge' is 'the repayment of some wrong, injury, etc. by the inflicting of hurt or harm.' That I like quite well," Maud had said. "And I also like that *revenge* is in the next column to *revelation* which is the act of disclosure. 'God's disclosure of Himself and His Will to His creatures.' Which must mean that He is disclosing to you that you've got to get this over with."

Will did write a play about Jamey's death called *Bitter Desire* and the Abbey did a reading of several drafts, but he never got the theme of revenge right and so there was, as Maud said, "no catharsis."

"You ought to come away from a play like that feeling better," she said. "And you come away feeling worse."

Now, seated across from Michael Maguire in the dimly lit room smelling of furniture polish, Will knew the definition of *revenge*. The world fell away, easily blown down by weather, and he sat in the center with his enemy, uncomplicated by distractions. Will Huston had never known such simple clarity of feeling except when Jamey died.

"You know I left Belfast when I was twenty-two and moved to London?"

"I do remember that," Will said. "You had just finished university."

Michael Maguire leaned forward a little awkwardly, his fleshy torso caught in the depth of the down sofa.

"Whiskey?" he asked.

Will considered.

"Red wine, please," he said. He took a handful of goldfish.

"Were we in university together?" Michael asked, pouring himself a glass of whiskey.

"You were in Belfast and I was in Dublin."

Michael Maguire had small watery eyes set close to the bridge of his nose, and his red hair fell in thin clumps across his forehead. He had an odd mouth, narrow and straight, as if it had been sewed on with dark thread in a perfect line. He did not seem capable of much activity, although Will sensed immediately that he was alert to this encounter and wary of it.

"Priscilla tells me you were not a priest when we knew each other." He filled Will's glass. "The only priest I knew was a rather loose-tongued Father Aidan who used to take on the university students at darts at Jack the Ripper's Pub."

"It was at Jack the Ripper's we knew each other," Will said.

"And you were not a priest?" Michael Maguire folded his clean, blushed hands on one knee.

"I was not," Will said. "I read law at Trinity College but my family is from Belfast."

There was only one lamp by the couch, which cast the living room in shadow, bringing with it a kind of silence even though they were speaking in normal voices. Michael turned on a small lamp with an Oriental base.

"You know, I used to go to Jack the Ripper's on weeknights with my friends from university, and there were others, probably Catholics from Falls Road, working class—they weren't in university."

"Exactly," Will said. "I came with my friends and it was quite a good drunken time we had." He took a sip of wine, careful not to drink too quickly, which he was inclined to do, to keep an edge.

"Your face doesn't look familiar, I'm terribly sorry to say, but then I am at heart a bureaucrat." He laughed, a throaty cigarette sound. "An executioner without a good memory for faces."

"We knew each other the summer of 1969. In fact, I was the only one who was Catholic and from Falls Road civilized by a university education, so you and I had quite a lot of talks since you were reading law as well."

There was an alteration in Michael Maguire's expression, not exactly alarm but suspicion, his mind spinning slowly around the turntable of his past.

"I remember one conversation we had in particular," Will continued. "It was about a girl to whom you were attracted—a little red-haired tart of a girl."

A memory of actual conversation had floated into Will's mind, a whole scene from Jack the Ripper's Pub which he had not thought about for years came to him now urged by the proximity of Michael Maguire, the familiarity of his cool wet eyes. Will was sitting at Jack the Ripper's with Brendan and a friend of Brendan's from technical school called Liam and Liam's girl, a pouty, pretty, red-haired girl, the kind that can make a man long for something he would be sorry to have—when Michael Maguire, a little drunk, sat down across the wooden table.

"So drinks all round," Michael said to the waiter, slapping a two-pound note on the table. "And some rose water for the beauty."

"Rose water?" the girl, who had not been introduced, said.

"To keep you lily pure, my love," Michael Maguire said, his voice a little slurred. He took her hand and put her fingers in his mouth.

"My gawd," the girl said pulling her fingers away from him, linking her arm through Liam's. But she was pleased with the attention of the university man.

"Let's get outta here," Liam said to the girl, who turned as she was leaving, Liam's arm around her waist, and blew a feather kiss from the end of her fingers to Michael.

"Don't you have your own girl?" Brendan asked. "Or do you only like the ones belonging to someone else?"

"You Catholics are too hot-tempered," Michael Maguire said to Brendan, rising from the bench and, as he did, pouring the remaining beer in the pitcher on Brendan's head.

"Do you remember Brendan Mallory?" Will asked.

"Brendan Mallory." Michael Maguire leaned forward on the couch. "I do remember Brendan Mallory. He was a cheeky man with dark red hair and a tendency to fight."

"That's right," Will said.

"In fact, I remember him very well." He sat forward on the couch, took a drink of whiskey. It was clear to Will by the set of his jaw, the sudden expression in his watery eyes, that he had mistaken the agenda for this evening.

"I remember now," he said. "And you were a friend of Brendan's."

Will could see by the watch on Michael's freckled wrist that it was between six-fifteen and six-twenty, so he needed to rush the moment to its conclusion before Priscilla Maguire arrived.

"I am his cousin," Will said, moving to the edge of the chair as if such confession required action.

"There were so many men," Michael Maguire said, a little dreamily. "And I left that summer, in late August, for London. I never came back."

"I'd wondered what had become of you in London," Will said. "I never heard again."

"I took a flat and got an entry-level job with the government. I only came back when my mother died in 1983 and then my father the next year." He picked up the bottle of whiskey to pour another glass and thought better of it.

"You left rather out of the blue," Will said. "I don't recall you'd said anything about going to London." The tone in his voice was cool but the adrenaline was surging, taking his breath away. Will looked at Michael Maguire in the gray light of early evening, looked at the pale thin skin of his cheeks, the blue veins laced in patterns just under the skin, the way he held his mouth in a line above his chin which receded into the pink flesh of his neck, his skin expanded to the limit of its elasticity—like a plump wood tick burrowing under the skin stretched to capacity with human blood.

"We talked once at Jack the Ripper's about appearances," Will said with a confidence which surprised him. "I remember specifically."

"Oh God. I was always so high-blown in my youth," Michael Maguire said.

"You said appearance is reality." Will moved forward with a strange excitement, not certain whether the story was a real memory or an invention on the spot. "And I said don't be foolish. Only God knows reality."

"You remember such lines so exactly after all these years?" Michael asked.

"Since I learned to speak, I have always been a memorizer of lines," Will said. "And you said, full of sarcasm, God? Who on earth is God?"

"And you said?" Michael Maguire asked, uncomfortable in the room now, agitated, listening for Priscilla. "Was that the door?" he asked. "Priscilla should be home at any moment."

"Do you remember Will Huston?" Will asked. "Brendan Mallory's cousin Will Huston?"

"I don't," Michael said, but there was a sudden rabbit terror in his eyes. He did remember. Surely he remembered.

"Then," Will leaned forward almost to Michael Maguire's face, speaking with an actor's sense of timing like perfect pitch, "you must remember Jamey Huston whom you killed on the thirteenth of July 1969."

Michael Maguire scrambled up from the couch.

"I am not the person you think I am," Michael Maguire said.

"You are the person exactly," Will said.

Will did not think what to do next; it simply happened that he grabbed Michael Maguire by the neck, throwing him down on the couch, his fat body squirming beneath him like a beetle, his face red.

"Do you remember now?" Will asked, his face almost against Michael's fleshy cheeks. "Say you remember."

"I remember," Michael said. "I remember now."

"It was a beautiful sunny day, remember?" Will said spitting the words on his face.

Michael tried to shake his head, firmly in Will's grip.

"I had parked my car across from Brendan's where I

was going for lunch with my little brother—James Aidan Patrick—that was his christening name, Quinn for my mother's family—Huston. James Aidan Patrick Quinn Huston, if you read the story in the Belfast paper on the following day. Did you read it? Did you read about what you had done or were you too yellow?'' Will had Michael's arms pinned with his knees, his hands around his neck, sitting on his chest, and he felt an ease about holding him there. He had a strength he'd never known in his life, as if he could kill several men with his bare hands.

''Talk,'' he said to Michael who was having difficulty breathing.

''I remember.''

''You were coming up the road toward Brendan's flat with a lot of cronies—and stupid as I was, I thought we would have a party on this sunny day, until Brendan said to me, 'Wait'—and who was it said 'Get in your houses'? Who was it said that? 'Get in your houses or you'll be shot'?''

''Please,'' Michael Maguire said. ''You are hurting me.''

''I mean to hurt you, Mr. Maguire,'' Will said. ''I mean to kill you. Do you remember who said that?''

''I said it,'' Michael said closing his eyes.

''And I was walking across the road with Jamey, close enough to recognize you. Michael Maguire, I said to myself. That red-haired Godless loyalist I see at Jack the Ripper's. There's Michael Maguire, I thought, carrying a pistol

—like the one I've got in my pocket right now, Mr. Maguire.'' He squeezed Michael's throat in his hands and his eyes seemed to pop out of their sockets. He loosened his grip.

"Can you hear me, Mr. Maguire?" He spit on his face. "Are you dead yet?"

"I hear," Michael said in a whisper.

"I recognized you on the street in Belfast," Will said. "What did you see when you looked at me?"

"Nothing," Michael said.

"Nothing?" Will asked. "You shot at nothing?"

"I shot at a man," Michael said.

"You shot at a boy," Will said. "You killed a little boy."

"I didn't mean to."

"You didn't mean to." Will tightened his grip on Michael Maguire's fleshy neck. It would be easy to kill him. He had no need of the revolver in his pocket, no desire for an impersonal act when his hands on Michael's throat were equal to the occasion. "You meant to kill the man, is that what you are telling me?"

Michael nodded.

"If I was close enough to know you, then you were close enough to know me," Will said.

Michael Maguire could no longer talk. His eyes, half open, had rolled back in his head, his tongue was out, hanging like a small squid over his lips.

"It was not an accident," Will said. He had a firm

hold on Michael Maguire's neck when they slid off the couch onto the hardwood floor beyond the carpet and Will banged his head again and again until, dangling from his neck, it no longer could be lifted from the floor. "It was not an accident," Will shouted. "It was not an accident. You saw me. You saw my little brother. You knew who I was. You knew me." He was out of control, shaking Michael until it looked as if his head would roll across the floor. "You shot Jamey intentionally and if you don't die on this evening, Michael Maguire, I will be back. I will be in your life forever, in your dreams day and night, until you do die."

Will squeezed his neck with the full strength of his hands—the lamp on the table behind him fell over so Will could no longer see Michael's face but he heard the front door, as if through a long tunnel or in a dream. And he heard the voice of a woman.

"Michael?"

Will's hands tightened on Michael Maguire's neck.

"I'm home," Priscilla Maguire called. "Michael?"

For a moment, Will thought that he would run. He jumped up, dropping the limp body of Michael Maguire so his head was propped against the leg of the coffee table. But when he heard her footsteps on the hardwood floor of the vestibule, he changed his mind. "Mrs. Maguire," he said when she appeared in the doorway, his voice surprisingly calm.

the counter when he answered the phone, trusting in the impeccable behavior of priests. An item on Page C1 caught his attention.

> Boy, 7, killed by Metro Bus
> Aaron Saile, age 7, a student at Lafayette School, was killed by a Metro bus at 5 P.M. yesterday at Pinehurst Circle when he ran in front of the bus to save his golden retriever puppy who escaped unharmed. . . .

Will did not read on about the boy or his small list of accomplishments or his parents or his family but an immediate and terrible anger came over him, a sudden anger like seasickness, and he wanted to kill a stranger—now the sleepy policeman whose head was against the silver rail so his hat tilted comically to one side. He clenched his teeth, unconsciously, drew his hands into a tight fist feeling the motion of hitting, of throwing the policeman on his back and pounding his florid face until pockets of flesh lay in soft deflated balloons around his cheeks. Will's hands were perspiring and he felt as if his disguise was askew.

He looked over at the policeman who had noticed Will but showed very little interest.

"Do you happen to know which stop to the Capitol?" he asked the policeman, although he knew, had planned to get off at Union Station to look at the shops, walk around the city, as he had hours to kill.

"What happened?" she asked, and seeing her husband on the floor, whispered, "What's happened to Michael?"

"What happened is this," Will said quietly. "Michael Maguire killed my little brother on the thirteenth of July 1969 in Belfast. I knew Michael then, as I told you yesterday. He saw me. He saw me walking across the street holding Jamey's hand and he killed him anyway."

She leaned against the door, her hands over her mouth.

"Did you kill Michael?"

Will looked down at Michael Maguire, struggling to move.

"I don't believe so," he said. "But I hope I have ruined his life." And Will walked into the kitchen, out the back door, down the steps of the high deck, out the gate, leaning against the alley side of the fence for just a moment to catch his breath. At the end of the alley he thought he saw someone, a woman perhaps. But when he looked again she was gone.

He took off the cassock, his gray wig, took the revolver out of his pocket and wrapped it in the priest's robe, undid the tie around a green trashbag in the trashbin two doors down from the Maguires', put the lid down. Then, exhilarated, wings on his feet, he ran down the alley toward Wisconsin Avenue.

24

Annie had lost him again. He climbed into the Diamond taxicab in front of Lacey House and there was no taxi for her to follow him, although she ran down R stopping at 21st and watched his cab turn on 22nd to Massachusetts. He did not have baggage, she thought, so he couldn't possibly be on his way to Dulles Airport where the last plane for Dublin was Aer Lingus and departed at nine-thirty P.M.— she had checked. She ran down R to 22nd and down 22nd to Massachusetts. Although many cabs passed her, it was rush hour and they were full of passengers. At Massachusetts, she found a taxi just as it stopped to let out another passenger.

"Where to?" the driver asked—a young bony man

with a cap of curly hair, egg yolk yellow hair that made her wonder if he dyed it such an unlikely color and if someone, a woman perhaps, liked the color and insisted. And had there ever been anything that Adam liked about her—the way she walked very straight like a dancer, the shape of her face—he had mentioned that once. What a funny thing to like about a person. But nothing else that she could remember in fifteen years.

"Where to, lady?" the driver asked again when the car behind him began to honk.

"I'm not sure yet," Annie said.

The taxi pulled into traffic. "Well, you probably ought to give it some thought," the driver said.

"I know. I know," Annie said, thinking quickly. So, if he had not gone to Dulles, since certainly he would have needed a suitcase for that, and if he were in fact leaving today for Dublin as he had told her at the café, then he was probably going to buy something to take back or tell someone good-bye.

"If you don't mind a scenic trip down Massachusetts Avenue toward Maryland," the driver said.

"Just a sec," Annie said. As for the places she knew he could be, he had either gone to Catholic University— but already he had been at Catholic University today—or else perhaps the house on Reservoir Road where she had seen him on two occasions. That seemed the most reasonable possibility.

"Reservoir Road please," she said, "the thirty-five hundred block of Reservoir Road."

And there he was walking up the front steps of the house with dying white petunias—as if she and her priest were doomed to be together, chosen by God, their fates locked in the stars, woven in the fabric of the universe. She wanted to sing right there in the taxicab—sing for this funny yellow-haired driver who was looking at her with the kind of impatience reserved for the demented. Sing for her beloved priest standing on the porch ringing the doorbell of 3524 Reservoir Road.

"I'm glad you're in such a good mood," the driver said, amused.

"I am. I am," Annie said. "It is absolutely crazy but I am."

"It appears pretty crazy," the driver said reaching back to take the money Annie was handing him.

"Keep the change," Annie called, waving gaily to the driver as if they were good friends.

She sat down on the steps of the house directly across the street and opened her green canvas bag, a large one from the Gap with one compartment into which she'd stuffed her passport, her hairbrush and wallet, a picture she always carried of Alexandra and Nicholas, her favorite, sitting side by side on the front steps of the house on Fessenden—Lexa like a Victorian child, her hands folded in her lap, her long hair in ribbons, and Nich-o beside her, his arm around her neck, one shoe on, and Brunnhilde precariously on his lap. She kissed the picture, kissed them each, one after the other, then checked her bag—a nightgown, her mustard yellow skirt and heavy navy turtleneck sweater for the damp, cold Irish autumn, a pair of jeans, two turtlenecks, socks, bikini underpants, her best—one burgundy-colored with a matching bra—and the red cloth hat. She wished she had packed her plum-colored skirt which was straight and made her look taller; although she had packed toiletries, even EMMA perfume, she had forgotten shampoo.

It had not once occurred to Annie Blakemore that when she presented herself to the priest, her actual self— Dolores Ann Grainey from Brammel, Texas—he might not be pleased to have her accompany him to Dublin. She was by temperament too much a believer in her own dreams, too passionate in her pursuit of him to entertain any doubt.

There was a light wind cracking the branches overhead, blowing her hair, but she sat on her canvas bag on the steps across from the house into which the priest had disappeared, this time with a plumpish red-haired man, and waited, her arms tight around her knees, her hat pulled down to her eyes, and as she waited she was singing, over and over in her mind, "Love O Love O Careless Love" and, not knowing any other verses, she sang to herself in the corner of her mind, "Love O Love O Faithful Love."

. . .

She was grown up, at Northwestern, the only Grainey child to go to college at all except Tom Boy, the Baptist minister in Waco, and home for summer vacation after her freshman year—surprised at how pleased she was to see them all except Rebecca, especially Ace, whose delight in her return kept him from regular afternoons at the pool hall, kept him a little sober.

On one of the breathlessly hot days of July, just around the Fourth, a Sunday after church, lunch cooked up by Rebecca and Athalia, Annie chopping onions and celery for the tuna fish and Billy Joe, twenty years old but small as a child, dancing to the music on the radio. "Love O Love O Careless Love."

"Love O Love O Faithful Love," Ace sang, taking Annie's hand, dancing with her.

"Stop that dancing, Ace," Rebecca said.

"On a Sunday, Papa," Athalia said.

"Love O Love O Foolish Love," Ace sang, doing a little awkward half step, whooping with delight. "Love O Love O Faithful Love," he sang, swinging Annie's hand as they danced around the kitchen.

"If you're going to sing with the radio," Rebecca said crossly, "sing the words the radio is singing or you ruin my nerves."

"Love O Love O Faithful Love," Ace sang. "That is what I long to have."

That night in Brammel, Rebecca upstairs with her Bible stories or her articles on self-improvement, Billy Joe watching television, Annie sat down with Ace in the kitchen drinking beer. She was nineteen that summer, too thin from working at McDonald's on the night shift to pay for school, braces on her teeth from the money she earned at Al's body shop working summers painting cars so she could sing with decent-looking teeth. But pretty—"Pretty as a picture," Andrew Fergusen in the senior class at Northwestern had told her when he kissed her good night. "So pretty to look at even with those wires on your teeth," Billy Hollis had told her when he ran his hands down her shirt, over her belly, and kissed her breast. "Almost beautiful," Adam Blakemore had said to her the first time they went out after the closing of *Holy Water,* in which he'd played a priest. "You are almost beautiful, Annie," he had said kissing her on the neck.

"What is faithful love to you, Papa?" Annie had asked Ace that night sitting across the Formica kitchen table from him in the dim light of evening.

"Faithful love is not something I have known, Dolores Ann," he said, taking her seriously. "But I think of it as what can happen between two people when they take off their disguises."

"And you have not had a faithful love with Mama?" Annie asked. "She has surely been faithful to you."

"No, she has not," Ace said. "Rebecca is faithful only to God and I to drink." He lifted his glass in a gesture of toasting. "Drink and God are the sad disguises of our marriage," he said. "And you, Dolores Ann, have so many disguises, it is not possible to know where one ends and you begin."

Annie laughed, reached over, and finished Ace's beer.

"So there's no chance for me to have a faithful love o love o faithful love," she sang.

"Who knows?" Ace said shrugging. "If you don't miss your chances."

The woman whom Annie had seen the previous morning at the house on Reservoir Road got out of her dark green BMW, locked the door, and went up the front steps of her house—a small square woman dressed cheerfully in a lilac suit. She unlocked her front door and went in the house just at the moment that a taxi, empty or so it seemed from the steps where Annie was sitting, turned down the alley where the day before she had watched the priest checking trashcans, and she suddenly wondered if the taxi had been called for him, a man with such an interest in trashcans, to go to the back of the house and pick him up in the alley. So she flung the canvas bag over her shoulder and followed the taxi, which was moving slowly, down the side alley where it turned left along the backs of the row houses and then picked up, driving too fast to stop for a passenger waiting in the alley. But as she stood at the alleys' intersection the priest, or it seemed in the dusk to be him, a man certainly and in a long black dress, came over the back fence and crouched by a large green trashcan. Annie ducked behind a fence, peering out so she could see him and hoping she could not be seen.

He did the most peculiar thing. She could not tell exactly what he was doing because he was almost twenty yards ahead, but what she thought she saw was the priest unbuttoning the front of his cassock and taking it off over his head. Then he walked away from her, a short distance, took something out of his pocket, wrapped it in the cassock, took something off his head, lifted the lid of a trash-can, pulled out a green plastic bag, untied the top, stuffed the cassock into the green bag, tied it, closed the lid, and set off down the alley toward Wisconsin Avenue in ordinary trousers and a dark sweater, walking briskly in the rain, not looking back.

She followed, keeping about a block behind, but it was necessary for her to occasionally run on the slippery street to keep up, down Wisconsin Avenue, past the café where she had first introduced herself to him, left on P Street, down the long blocks of row houses, past the entrance to Rock Creek Park, the restaurants, the small shops, to Dupont Circle. At People's Drug he went inside and she waited at the corner, her beret pulled down, although he could, she suppose, recognize her from the subway. She was out of breath, wet to the bone from the thin rain, but she kept her eyes directed at the door to People's in case she should miss him now he had gotten rid of his black robe.

So was he not a priest? she wondered, her heart beating with what had suddenly appeared to be a dangerous chase—although she was exhilarated by this discovery, not frightened, not even worried that this priest might not be what he seemed, might be, in fact, an ordinary man. If so, she thought to herself, keeping her eyes on the main entrance to People's, he was on a mission or he would not find the need for a disguise, just as she was on a mission. So they had something in common.

He came out with a brown paper bag, a newspaper rolled under his arm, and she saw immediately that his hair was no longer gray, but black and long, falling across his forehead.

The subway headed toward Silver Spring was crowded with late rush hour traffic so Annie stood next to him, stood so close, although her back was to him, that occasionally their bodies touched, his thigh next to hers, and she imagined turning toward him, taking him in her arms. She wondered had the lines of appropriate behavior suddenly disappeared and could she be in the act of doing what she had only imagined, like laughing in church when she was small. And was he a priest, was her attraction only to the fact that he was a priest, or did that feeling of electricity come from himself and not simply the cassock he was wearing?

At Union Station she stood in line for tickets several people behind him but she heard him ask the man at the counter for the next train to New York City.

"The eight-thirty Colonial," the man said.

"I'll take a one-way ticket please," he said. He put his ticket in his pocket and headed toward the wall of the station where the telephones and lockers were located.

"One way to New York City," Annie said taking out her wallet, handing the man her Visa card. When she walked into the main hall of the station, the clock over the gates said seven-fifty, so she had plenty of time to call Clementine. Across the hall she could see the priest standing beside the lockers, so she waited until he had opened one and taken out a small knapsack before she went to the telephones to call Dallas. So he had not planned to leave from Dulles after all, she thought. Perhaps he was flying to Dublin from New York. There was no reason to think he would be going from Dulles necessarily since he had only said he was going to Dublin. If, of course, he was the person he had been at the café on Wednesday.

Annie slid into the telephone cubicle and dialed Clementine.

"So," Clem said. "We've had a wonderful day. Sylvie loved the perfume and Alexandra has promised to go back to see her next visiting day which is Tuesday and when we left Sylvie cried. I don't think I've ever seen Sylvie cry, even during the trial. And it's all because of your blessed children."

"That's lovely," Annie said, distracted, for she had lost track of the priest. She had seen him leave the news kiosk and now he was gone.

"So we're making popcorn and then we're going to watch *Otello* on the VCR. Nicholas says it is his second favorite after *Aida*. So here they are." And Annie talked to each of the children.

"Are you at home now?" Clementine asked when she came back on the line.

"No, Clem, I'm not," Annie said. "I'm on my way to New York, and Adam is safe with his mother in Connecticut. I'll call you as soon as I get to New York and let you know where I'm staying."

"New York," Clementine said. "For what reason would you be going to New York?"

"Remember I mentioned the priest," Annie said.

"It's unlikely I should forget, Dolores Ann."

"Well, I am going to New York with him. It's a sort of ecumenical thing."

"Ecumenical?"

"Religious." She decided not to tell Clementine just yet that he no longer seemed to be a priest.

"Well, behave yourself and—Dolores Ann—do you take vitamins?"

"Not unless I'm pregnant. Should I?"

"You should get vitamin E right away for your heart," Clementine said.

"I promise," Annie said.

After she hung up the telephone, she searched in the canvas bag for her red cloth hat, the one she had worn the first time she saw the priest on the subway. She took off the black beret, stuffed it in her bag, and put on the red hat. Then she called Sara Ponder to tell her that the key to the house was under the doormat, to please feed Siegfried and Brunnhilde and leave lights on in the living room and the upstairs bedroom and the porch. She bought a small bottle of vitamin E and shampoo at the pharmacy and *Good House-keeping* at the newsstand.

The eight-thirty train was surprisingly crowded. Annie got on late, on the first car, walking through slowly checking the passengers. If the priest had not gotten on the train, she decided, had not planned to leave Washington at all, had suspected she was following him and did not wish to be discovered as an ordinary man, then she would get off in Baltimore and return by the next train.

She went through the first car, which was the club car, and then a coach car and the food service car where the line was already forming. The fourth car was particularly crowded with people in the aisles, putting their luggage and coats in the overhead racks.

She saw him at the very end of the fourth car. He was lifting a small piece of luggage to the rack above the last seat in the car. Then he sat down. She moved between the passengers, taking deep breaths as she had been told to do by Clementine and the children's pediatrician and even Adam if ever she felt the coming of a panic attack.

He was facing away from her, facing the door to the next car, in a seat for four people, but the other seats were empty. The newspaper was open on his lap and his feet were up on the seat directly across from him.

"Excuse me," she said lifting her skirt, stepping over his legs just as he moved them away. "Do you mind if I sit down?"

"Not at all," he said without looking up.

25

The train lurched forward and began its slow crawl into the darkness sprinkled with city lights. The priest had the newspaper open but Annie could see him, could see the sharp angles of his slender face, the olive green eyes she had noticed the first afternoon on the subway; he looked just like himself, which was to say just as he had looked as a priest, except for the black hair and the absence of the reddish scar on his cheek. But without his cassock, he was an ordinary man. Or was he, she wondered, a figure of romance only in the robes of a Roman Catholic priest?

She opened *Good Housekeeping,* skipping the recipes to a story about a miracle baby, keeping the priest's face in view so she could see him without appearing to be looking. She wished she had chosen another magazine besides *Good Housekeeping,* although she did love to read the recipes, not necessarily to cook the brightly colored meals pictured on the pages but just to read the recipes for a kind of comfort that the lists of names of food gave her, and she liked the stories of domestic drama closer to the librettos of operas than the small, elegant stories of *The New Yorker,* for example—she was explaining in her mind these observations to the priest in case he questioned her choice of magazines. To be certain he did not misunderstand her, she took *Così Fan Tutte* out of her bag and put it on the train seat beside her.

Will Huston could not settle down. He had walked all the way to Dupont Circle, almost run, through the city streets just for the exhilaration of the damp air, the wet November air on his cheeks, a sense of triumph spurring him on.

He wanted to tell someone. The elderly man, well dressed and serious in appearance, he passed on P Street. "How do you do?" he wanted to say. "You are speaking to a man who has just avenged his brother's death."

"How do you do, Mum?" he wanted to say to the woman, like his mother could have been, fit and substantial, who stood beside him waiting for the light on 20th Street. "I have just frightened—actually," he'd correct himself—"terrified the man who killed my little brother." He felt a sense of extraordinary strength and weightlessness, as if he were a large bird, airborne, fearless in descent.

"Hello," he wanted to say to the pretty woman, his age, perhaps a little younger, buying Tylenol and a candy bar in the line at People's Drug. "I want to tell you a story if you have a moment to listen."

Will wanted to be acknowledged—not in a grand manner by any means, not with any significance; his time in Washington had been, after all, a private journey—but he wanted to tell someone the story of what had happened in Michael Maguire's parlor as if only in the telling could the story become true.

At Union Station, he called Brendan saying he'd be back in New York City about midnight and was scheduled for a plane to Dublin on Saturday, but who could tell? Uncle Patrick had been fit enough but suffering from senility and did not know him. Then he bought a detective novel at the newsstand, a pack of cigarettes, a box of chocolate-covered peanuts, and a beer which he drank waiting for the announcement to be posted under Departures that his train was boarding.

In the train, he chose an empty seat with four places, two and two, facing each other. And just as he was settling in to read the newspaper, a young woman whose red cloth hat shielded her face stepped over him, a nervous woman—he could feel the conversation rushing in her brain even before she asked if she could sit down.

The conductor was a small gruff man who seemed to be in an uneven humor. "One way to New York City," he said tearing the ticket, giving Will the stub and a seat check. "Are you together?" he asked, taking Annie's ticket.

"Separate," Will said.

"Alone," Annie said quickly.

"Well, keep your feet off the seat, sir," the conductor said to Will crossly. "We try to keep these seats clean."

Will put his head against the seat back and waited until the conductor had moved on to the next car and then he looked at Annie, with a rush of blood to his head, a heat in his belly, knowing that this woman in the red hat was the same woman in the black beret and she had followed him now to the train.

"Who are you?" he asked quietly.

But she could not respond. As she waited for the conductor to collect her ticket, she had felt the slow ascent of panic. Her lungs deflated, her breath thinned to a slender ribbon of oxygen caught in her throat, and she couldn't breathe. She tried to swallow and could not, tried to speak. She dropped the magazine on the floor beside her and sat up very straight to lengthen her torso, to make room for air, breathing through her nose, small, shallow, unsuccessful breaths.

"Are you all right?" Will asked.

Annie shook her head. It felt to her as if she were weeping but there were no tears.

Will put down his newspaper.

"Can I do something?" he asked. "Would you like a glass of water?"

Annie nodded, lightheaded now, fearful she would faint, or die, on the Amtrak train in the company of strangers.

Will got a flimsy paper cup from the dispenser next to the rest rooms, punched the button, and filled the cup with water, and then, as if it were the most natural gesture on earth, he put the cup to her lips and she drank it, breathing more easily again.

"Thank you," she said leaning back against the seat. "Sometimes I get these panic attacks out of nowhere, washing over me, and I feel as if my mechanism for breathing has broken down." She rubbed her eyes with the back of her hand, spreading mascara across her cheek. "I'm sorry to have bothered you."

Will folded his newspaper and put it on the seat beside him.

The train had passed New Carrollton traveling out of the city lights, forty minutes away from Baltimore, so he could not leave voluntarily unless he jumped. Annie picked up *Good Housekeeping,* stuffed it in her bag, and tucked her feet under her long skirt.

"I had thought you were a priest," she said.

The lights had been dimmed in the coach car, the train had picked up speed, flying through the night; it was difficult to hear above the racketing of metal against metal on the tracks.

Will stalled for time. "You thought I was a priest?"

"You were a priest. Just a little while ago, I saw you." She drew her legs up under her chin. "You had gray hair and a black cassock."

Will shook his head. "I think you have mistaken me for someone else," he said.

"No, I couldn't have," Annie said. "I saw you first on the subway from Union Station to Dupont Circle on Tuesday at about four-thirty in the afternoon," she said. "And you were in a cassock then with quite long gray hair and a scar on your face." Her cheeks were hot, her hands, damp from perspiration, were slippery. "And I sat down."

"Beside me?" He would try to make a joke of it, he thought, pretend his priestliness was a folly of her own and he had not been on the subway. But he remembered now, remembered her exactly, that Spanish dancer was how he had thought of her at the time, with her fine carriage and the same red hat she had on now.

"You don't remember," Annie said. "I thought you might."

"I don't," Will said. "I don't remember you at all."

He seemed quite different to Annie now than the priest had seemed when she saw him this morning and yesterday at the café. Perhaps she had been mistaken and

the man she'd seen dump his cassock in the trash was another man whom she'd lost in the pursuit. She could even
have forgotten the look of the priest on the subway, the
color of his eyes, the way his hands were shaped. "When
you got off the subway, I followed you," she said.

He was going to think she was unstable, following a
priest off a subway, and she had been unstable, she thought.
She was. Adam's mother had been right about insanity in
the Grainey family. Certainly Ace would be described by a
professional in the field of mental illness as a troubled man.

"You followed me?" he asked.

"I followed you off the subway and down R Street to
the house where you were staying, 2115. You probably hate
to hear this news," she said.

"Are you in the habit of following people?" Will
asked, disarmed.

"I've never followed anyone before," Annie said.
"But I have always had an interest," she began. "More
than an interest, I suppose. More like an obsession—my
mother would have called it—an obsession with priests."
She unfolded her hands, took off her red hat, and her long
hair fell around her face. "And there you were in the subway, looking sort of wonderful." She laughed. "Maybe not
even a priest." She ran her hands through her hair. "Something happened to me and I felt as if I had to follow you."

"What did you think would possibly come of it?"
Will asked. An unfamiliar feeling rushed to the surface of
his body as if he were in a state of permanent blushing. So

there he had been slinking through Washington, D.C., covering his tracks, taking every possibility of discovery into consideration. He had even believed himself. And all the time he had been discovered already, followed by this slip of a girl.

Annie shrugged.

"I didn't think about what would come of it in my actual life," Annie said. "I suppose it suddenly occurred to me, what if?" She looked over at him. "I imagine you think I'm crazy," she said.

Will was beginning to feel out of breath himself, attacked by nerves, in a way familiar, like stage fright or the unbridled excitement of a young man alone for the first time with a woman in the shadows of a private place. She was lovely to look at, he thought, the planes of her face, her small chin and long slender neck.

"And I thought to myself, of course," Annie said. "I'll just do what I imagine doing. So on Wednesday morning, after I had seen where you lived, I got up very early and put on my favorite brown hat." She laughed. "I have worn hats ever since I left home." She crossed her legs under her corduroy dress. "I followed you to a house on Reservoir Road where you were visiting a woman and then to a café where I spoke to you." She looked over at him. "Are you beginning to remember me now?"

"I think I am," Will said. And he felt as if he had known this odd young woman in some part of himself locked away, like childhood secrets whose knowledge brings too much pure sadness.

"At the café, you said you could be of no assistance because you were leaving today for Dublin and I thought you'd be leaving from Dulles Airport, so I got up this morning—actually I didn't sleep at all last night—but I did follow you to Catholic University."

"Don't tell me," Will said beginning to laugh. "You followed me to the cafeteria in your black beret pulled down to your eyes." Will was laughing now, deep laughs rolling out of his stomach like sobs, as if the laughter would turn to weeping at any moment.

Annie nodded. "And then you disappeared," she said.

"I should have guessed that it was you," Will said reaching over, brushing a strand of her hair off her forehead.

"But you didn't know me," Annie said.

"I should have. I certainly should have," Will said.

"Baltimore," the conductor called out. "In about three minutes we will be arriving at Station Baltimore."

Will rested his chin in his hands. He had a peculiar sense he recalled from childhood when, looking in the mirror over the toilet, he had not recognized the reproduction of his own face, not known the features, the way his hair fell across his forehead, the expression in his eyes. Holding to that vision of a stranger, he used to invent other people to become for that moment, before he surfaced as himself again, William Huston, Will Huston of Belfast, of Arch-duke Street, Dublin, brother of Jamey Huston, dead at six, fixed forever in his mind as a child repeated in the faces of other children who would today, were Jamey living, be much younger than Jamey. The age of Nicholas.

Will felt unsteady, lightheaded, almost drunk, as if the events of the past three days had not just happened, but happened long ago at the time that Jamey died, and this new sense of himself, exploding with the feeling of a love affair—for wasn't this the way a love affair should feel?—had been in a permanent chrysalis for more than twenty years.

When the train slowed down arriving in Baltimore, the aisles filling with departing passengers, Will and Annie stopped speaking. Will picked up the newspaper and skimmed the national news and Annie, scrambling through the zipper pocket of her bag for her hairbrush, dumped out the contents—her passport, her wallet, her picture of Nicholas and Alexandra.

The train was filling up. An elderly woman short of breath started to sit down next to Annie but the man with whom she was traveling urged her on.

"You have pictures?" Will asked. He reached over to take the photograph in her lap.

"Do you mind?" he asked.

"Not at all." Annie smiled, putting her brush away.

"Your children?" he asked. "You look too young to be a mother."

"I'm quite old enough," she said.

Will looked at the picture under the reading light over his head, at the old-fashioned and familiar girl with her long hair and expression of nineteenth-century tranquillity, at the boy with an impish smile, his arm around his sister's neck. His heart sounded in his chest with such a force, as if it were the final beat his heart was going to take. Certainly he was not mistaken. He could not possibly mistake that wide-open face for another.

"Your children?" he asked and his voice was caught almost to silence in his throat.

Annie looked at him oddly. "Yes," she said. "They are visiting my sister in Dallas. Are you all right?"

He ran his hand through his hair and took a deep breath, nodding, although he did not feel all right.

"Nicholas and Alexandra," Annie said. "Russian names because I used to pretend I was Russian." She laughed. "I would say my name was Anna Tolstoy because there were a lot of Tolstoys in America so it seemed a safe choice and I gave my children grand names so they could grow into them, like being born with large eyes."

"I met your children at the opera," Will said. "I took Nicholas to the men's."

"You met my children?" Annie asked, the blood slipping from her face.

"I saw you sing Despina," Will said in a voice he did

not recognize as his own. "I had standing room in the opera and your children were there."

"My God," Annie said. She could not catch her breath. "And you talked to them."

"I talked to them both." Will looked out the window of the train at the darkness after Baltimore, not wanting to look at her. He started to tell her that Nicholas had reminded him of Jamey, even that he had been Jamey in the flesh these last hours, but he did not trust himself to speak without weeping.

"I'm very glad you talked to them," Annie said softly, not wishing to spoil the wonderful, unexpected strangeness of this moment.

"On Wednesday, I saw your children again at *Don Giovanni* and your husband was there."

Annie took the picture he handed her and put her wallet and hairbrush back in the bag.

"My children's father," she said. "Not my husband." Not my husband, she thought, not my responsibility, not my penance, not my husband any longer or forever. "Adam and I are separated," she said.

"I'm sorry," Will said, half aware of the conversation, still too stunned by the resurrection of the boy Nicholas, now his, now the child of this young woman whom he would follow to the end of the earth.

"It's not sad," Annie said. "We were unhappy." The train flew past the small towns of Maryland with streetlights flashing in the windows. Annie leaned toward him. "Now will you tell me, are you really a priest?"

"If I were, what would you want from me?" he asked.

She gave an embarrassed laugh, because there was something she wanted but it seemed such a foolish request. What she wanted was to make a confession and to be forgiven.

Crossing the bridge over the Susquehanna River, spread like thin glass between the trees, past Elkton and into Delaware, along the dark flat cornfields south of Wilmington, she told Will Huston about her family and Adam and the accident. As she spoke, the other passengers in the coach seemed to have vanished, the space beyond had fallen in shadow, and there was the illusion of light accumulating around her and Will.

"That is why I have been in search of priests," Annie said when she had finished her story.

"But you have done nothing for which to be forgiven," Will said.

"You don't think so?" Annie asked.

"Not that you have told me," Will said putting his feet up on the seat beside her.

"So now will you tell me your real name?" Annie asked.

"My name is Will Huston," Will said, "and I'm an actor with the Abbey Theatre in Dublin."

"You're not a priest at all?"

"I'm not," Will said.

"Then why were you pretending?" Annie asked.

"I'll tell you that story," Will said, "but we have to start at the beginning and since this is the beginning, you tell me your name."

"Dolores Ann Grainey," she said. "That is the name I was given when I was born."

Annie could feel in the movement of the air that something had happened between them. For this moment, perhaps only this moment on the train hurtling east, or maybe longer, maybe for her lifetime, she had the sense of going home.

And it seemed as if the train for New York City, traveling through the darkness of rural Delaware, sailed off the tracks then, bearing them above the farmlands of the eastern coast, above the cities, above the clouds and smog which disguised the heavens from the people on earth, and toward a canopy of stars.

About the Author

SUSAN RICHARDS SHREVE is the author of eight previous novels—among them, most recently, *Daughters of the New World, A Country of Strangers,* and *Queen of Hearts.* She has also written award-winning children's books and has contributed to several publications. In addition to writing she is a professor of English at George Mason University and can be seen from time to time as an essayist on PBS's "The MacNeil/Lehrer NewsHour." She lives in Washington, D.C.